HILLBILLY HYMN

HILLBILLY HYMN

A Faerie Tale

Peter Biles

RESOURCE *Publications* · Eugene, Oregon

HILLBILLY HYMN
A Faerie Tale

Resource Publications
An Imprint of Wipf and Stock Publishers
199 W. 8th Ave., Suite 3
Eugene, OR 97401

www.wipfandstock.com

PAPERBACK ISBN: 978-1-6667-4468-2
HARDCOVER ISBN: 978-1-6667-4469-9
EBOOK ISBN: 978-1-6667-4470-5

MAY 9, 2022 5:59 PM

For Cody Weaver

"No story ever really ends, and I think I know why."

— GEORGE MACDONALD

Prologue

T HIS here is a yarn which often I'm asked to spin around the wood burning stove or the campfire in town, and which for some reason or another, folks and kin liken to hear. It ain't for the faint of heart, I'll tell you that much. There's ghouls and ghosts and adventures and all manner of dangers in the following pages, but if there warn't, what's the point in telling it to folks? Ain't no one want to hear a story with no punch or pie to it, about some feller or other who just set on his couch watching TV programs. Ain't nobody want to set there and listen about folks who never set foot outside their parlor, waiting for the world to change! But anyway, if you've a spell to set yourself down and pay attention to my li'l neck of the woods, it may be worth your weight to go 'head and do it. There's something for everybody in this tale, whether you is of the hill country or not. But be wary if ye think it ain't worth the snuff to talk about people who ain't hitting it big in Wall Street nor Hollywood nor the White House. If ye want a story about fame or glamour or guys getting beautiful gals like they show on Coca Cola ads, ye ought to visit the movie houses. More exists in the hidden places of the world than in the assumptions of all the bigshots, and the wonders of the universe are oft held in somethin' as simple as a fall of snow in the woods . . .

CHAPTER ONE

COMES a time when a man's got to start tending his own and say to himself "enough is enough" and that breaking of the camel's back come to me that sorry old winter when my chickens started getting picked off one by one, stupid buggers that they are. Mindy, she blamed it on a little old bobcat, and I said: "Bobcat! Woman I been tendin' those chickens for twenty years and ain't seen no cowardly bobcat take my critters. You've seen my fencin.' This is somethin' bigger."

"Maybe they just ain't been around until now," she said, laying out the fixings for supper, and I peered out the window to see dusk shining its tones upon the chicken coop. Just a couple of hens pecked like a couple sad widows in the yard, well within the fence, and I said "bah!" and brewed some coffee while my dear Mindy called for the children to come on down and eat. Little Bobby is seven years old and eats like steer takes hay, and our sixteen-year-old Sammie eats like a lady and can't hardly stand the fellow gobbling up the table as he does. But she's got that old virtue of temperance, as the schoolteachers do say, according to Plato and somebody I hear they call 'Totle or something or other, so she forebears him and then helps me go out and feed the pups. After we did so, Sammie and I trudged on over to the chicken coop and I gave the chicken wire a heavy rundown from top to bottom and

1

couldn't detect nary a hole nor tunnel nor any other creaturely device.

"Shoot Daddy, I wonder what it could be, takin' them all," said Sammie.

"Ma thinks it's a bobcat, and God bless her but I must declare I believe that to be hog hoof," I said.

"What do you think it is?"

"Well, Sammie, you might think your old Pa has lost his alfalfa, but shoot, it looks like the work of Bigfoot. Look here. Tree over here bent plumb over. The feller done clumb up and snatched them up from above like a devil on Hallerween."

"Old Mister Tate yonder the ridge said he saw Bigfoot t'other day. Shem was tellin' me about it."

"Tate! He's got eagle eyes even if the bugger is as old as Methuselah, God love him. And Shem you say . . . who's this Shem I hear tell?"

"Just a boy from school."

"So Bigfoot and boyfriends both comin' to haunt my home. 'Tis the reckoning, or rapture, I'll be . . . "

Sammie blushed so I didn't say nothing more; she's a beauty of a young woman, and surely this Shem I hear about ain't so bad, it's just that I heard his name talked about in the same sentence as Bigfoot, so the name now comes across with some sour to it. You understand.

"What else did Tate say?"

"His goats are missin'. He ain't lost a goat in forty years. Except to natural causes, 'course."

"Man's old enough, that's no bluff. Old as Timbuktu if I could put a wager on him. Anyhow, is that right?"

"Yessir. Apparently, it's a real community dilemma."

"Well, I'll be derned." I kicked at some mushrooms which looked to be poisonous by the smell they wafted up and turned to look at my house.

"Maybe I'll phone old Tate and we'll just make a stakeout of it," I declared. "Pretty soon this here Bigfoot might be stealin' our families too, or worse, all that moonshine in Hogback Creek we got hid."

"Yessir. Bobby will wanna come 'long."

"It ain't an option. He'll have his chance here one of these days. Tate and me will take care of it this time around."

I told my plan to Mindy that night as we winded down from an evening of card games with the kiddos and I even struck a cigarette in the window to show her how serious I was.

"Bigfoot? C'mon, Arnie. You really think so?"

"Tate saw him with his own eyes, and don't remember that when I's just a pup of a boy—"

"—that you saw a big hairy man catch a bass with its bare hands over at Shady Ridge Creek and you said to yourself that day: 'well, that weren't no man a 'tall but some sort of ape we done learned about in archaeology today at school.'"

"Ah, you know the yarn, Mindy. But that don't mean it ain't true."

"You know how I feel about you goin' out alone at night. You remember what happened last time."

"Last time I WAS alone, Mindy, but I phoned Tate ten minutes ago and he's all fired up to shoot down this here Bigfoot, swears he seen him with his own eyes."

"Don't do it, Arnie. Don't worry me so about where your butt's gonna be in the morning."

"My butt's yours truly, always, darlin', but the farm's in danger and it ain't just us. Got more calls tonight about farm animals gettin' plucked."

Mindy was talking of the time I got cut up by a bunch of hogs after going out at night to see if I couldn't shoot the whole herd down, but those were in my stupid years, which you see the dear Lord above allows us to show us we're stupid; I ain't ever going out alone in the wilderness again and that's a promise I gave Mindy the day I limped on home from the Dr. Bernie's clinic. This is different. I don't tangle with Bigfoot lightly. I tangle with him arm in arm with a trusted brother and veteran of the woods. That's Tate. He's the sage of us all and prays so much you'd reckon the Holy Spirit drips off his breath like honey to sweeten the very ground beneath his feet. So you see I do believe the man when I hear him. And the man can shoot the ever-loving daylights out of the critters which come stirring trouble in his cornfield.

There are some Bigfeet out there who we'll call tame. A Bigfoot always reflects the country he comes from. That's the belief I take. So it follows the Bigfoot around here's got to be one tough bugger, clever and no doubt has a knack for kicking back with all his critter brethren and playing "flinch" and remembering the good old primordial days when we human beings warn't around yet. America used to be Bigfoot country, see, and they'd all roam free, but that all ended with Teddy Roosevelt's presidency when he made a decree that hunting the Sasquatch was legal and all. I can fetch a copy of the documentation but my reading eyes ain't tolerating much speculation at the moment. So they all went into hiding. As did the werewolves and a few witches and probably a few of them spirits which the good Lord won't permit me to mention in detail. But they're all out there spooking the world up. Just you go look out one starry night in November and see if you don't get a chill go down your spine, a chill which surely ain't due to the temperature. World's haunted, not just sinful, but you know we all walk around like it's purely a material place that's ours to tend. But it ain't. Not if I got anything to say about it.

Mindy went and sat down on the chest by the window as she does when she's sad and pensive (I always do say she should have married a poet 'stead of a poor old chicken farmer like me, but it swells my soul to hear her say "I choose ye, Arnie, over all the dead poets in the world"). She looked out into the crisp night as she does when she talks to God.

"Big, strange world, ain't it," she whispered, looking back at me. A funny thing, marriage. If you truly love the woman ye marry, you'll think she gets all the more beautiful as time performs its parade, not less. I go into town at times and see these Coca Cola ads with women drinking on the covers and they ain't got nary more than two stitches of clothing on them and I tend to say to myself, "Doggone, she don't even look like a real person hardly.

She's propped up like a statue like they got at the Parthenon over in the ancient country, except all she's there for is to get some guys buying a Coca Cola so they'll attract the womenfolk." But Mindy, I see her on that there windowsill and I perceive a real person there, soul breathing beauty into body, and that's all I need to know to swoon. We'll be lovers 'til we kick the can for that very reason.

"Well, Arnie, I love you something awful and I know old Tate's on his last leg. So maybe y'all should go. Make it a well way out for him."

"You know I'll blow my bear horn if we git in a fix."

"I know it."

And that was that. I done picked her up in my arms and carried her over to our corncob mattress by which a woodstove eternally crackles its vestiges upon our bodily abodes and we kept each other company and comfort the whole night through as some coyotes yipped at the moon down yonder in the thickets.

Next morning, I trudged on over to Tate's through a seven-inch fall of snow which had started something fierce in the middle of the night. The day was overcast and bitterly cold, so I blew into my mitts and down the throat of my coat. Some doe scattered in downy quiet before me, frighted no doubt by my four-gauge shotgun which I had slung across my back. I reached in a pocket and tore off some jerky with my teeth and ground on it. Tate's farm seeped into sight, the smell of goat crap lofting up to meet my heaving nostrils, but 'tis a right honorable smell so I couldn't think nothing but appreciation for it. Tate himself I spotted hunched like a first-century appendage over the hood of his tractor and cursing the radiator because I presume he'd got it frozen up during the night. Tate lives alone up here on the hill. He's lived alone up here for some fifty years, and though a strapping feller, ain't ever wooed no other farm gals for him to marry but stuck to solitude and became a right spiritual man because of it, claiming he missed the companionship of a woman something terrible but come to hearken on the Presence of the Lord in some profound way, he said. "Good Lord made these woods and everythin' in it," he told me. "Even the Bigfoots among them. But we can't have them stealin' our livelihood."

"Hello!" said I, and the old man spun around in vigilance and muttered, "Curse and travail you, Arnie Tuck! You done scared the corn pone out of me."

"Ho ho!" I said, and he snatched my hand and brought me into a bear hug so I remembered my old man whilst it lasted.

"So, ye've taken up the grand call," he said, nodding and tugging at a beard the shape of a cat's ear. Cats and dogs roamed the snow shodden grounds of the farm like curious wraiths, heads popped up over robes of white. He grunted and told me to get my butt indoors where coffee and corn pone was waiting.

"So it's stealin' all your goats, I hear tell," I said, taking a mug of coffee from him and as always when I visited admired his spread of taxidermy on the walls of the parlor. The only critter missing is a Bigfoot, I notice every time, but we aim to remedy that of course.

"That's what I ascertain," the old geezer proclaimed, taking out his pipe and smoking long trails of blue smoke into the air so the ceiling attracted a swirly haze like the house had a mind and was pondering the nature of our conversation. "But there ain't no tellin' for sure. Today's a good day to hunt. Snow'll bring out the tracks sure as shootfire."

Tate himself poured some whisky but didn't take much; he watched himself when it came to that sort of thing and joined me at the kitchen table with a cup of coffee, peering with his single green eye out into the wilder-capped world. He sniffed. "Went to the city a few days ago," he said. "Told my doctor Bigfoot was afoot and he got real concerned. Had me get one of them confounded X-rays and looked inside my head usin' some sonar deevice. He thought I was plumb crazy, Arnie. Told a nurse of his that these sorts of things tend to happen to we lonely hillbilly oldies. Bah! I got ears sharp as a fox cub's, they think I'm deafer n' the dead."

"Shoot, that's a shame, Tate. But I reckon it's good ye got your checkup."

"I reckon so. They give me a week to live, so I'll take it or leave it at that." He said it so casual-like that I nearly carried on the talk like it was nothing, but I stopped short and said, "One week?"

"That's right, son. But I suppose they don't know what the hell they're talkin' about. Always was suspicious of them folks, Lord love them."

"Shoot, Tate. I do wish I could help in some way."

"But ye are helpin' me. We're goin' on this here hunt and it's gonna lead me right to the pearly gates." He sipped and stared hard at the table. "Pearly gates," he repeated at a whisper. "Why they call them pearly I wonder? Don't say that in the Bible, I don't believe. Maybe it does. I don't know. Wonder why it can't be woody gates, or gates with my old creeks flowin' through them, gold and pearl enough when sun and moon shine on them."

"You're talkin' about home," I said. "You're very backyard."

"Home it is," he nodded, smiling. "You care fer a plot a land for sixty years and it becomes heaven enough. I don't believe I want to die after all, young buck." His hands of leather were trembling as they do because he's so doggone old, and for the time being we forgot all about Bigfoot. It was like we was just setting there with nary a plan at all. Just setting. And an hour went on by but we kept on talking about the upcoming spring and how crops were expected to do come harvest.

"Lord'll provide for you," Tate said. "Just do your part and bust your butt for your family."

"I know it. Ain't a Bigfoot around which can stop the Providence."

"Gospel truth."

"You think it's going to snow all the week long?"

"I reckon. Felt a pang in my shinbone this very mornin', and ye know that implies. Snow enough to hide a Yeti belongin' to them big old Himerlayas."

Snow kept fiddling on down like sweets on a sour surface, transfixing the woods in drapery and causing the figures of birds to bleed against the white. Tate does love watching them birds. He always says he could watch them for days on end think of that verse in Matthew where the good Lord speaks of speculating the birds and taking stock of their full bellies and happy chirping, how good it would be human beings too would put on their downright nature and chirp away all the troubles of life like chaff at the mill. Not to deny cold days like these, but to toss snow for joy in them, nonetheless. Tate whistled and wagged his head, muttering, "Could see the movement of a mouse in that kind of stillness. I think we'd have seen Bigfoot by now if he was clomping around here like we think he is."

"He may've moved North to meet up with his brethren," I hypothesized. "They do that from time to time. Have to reunite with their kind, you see."

"Truly that, son. It's gettin' on evenin' tonight. Ye'd better call your woman and tell her the snow's piling up somethin' dangerous with the dark." Tate don't boss nobody around but when he commands, he does it like it's just got to be so, no contestation invited. So, I went on over the phone on the wall, which got to be harvested from Graham Bell's closet of first drafts, let me tell you, and called my sweet honey as the snow turned torrential and we couldn't see the birds no more.

"Arnie, I'm sorry about Tate," Mindy crooned over the phone. "Stay with him. Keep him company. I love you, darlin.'"

"My love's all yours."

"Careful on your way home tomorrow."

We clicked our separate ways and I saw Tate had already mashed up some bedding for me on his leather couch which he had drug all the way from Shady Ridge. It's one of them in which you sink in deeper and deeper the longer the night lasts and you just stare into the coals of the fire until it's like Jesus himself soothes your soul to sleep.

"This'll keep you toasted," he said. We sat in the parlor and smoked, letting the silence get us real relaxed, and Tate's back porch light blared white so we saw the snow tumble and elevate against the glass of the door. Tate sipped a bit more whisky.

"Let's go on and look for the squatch tomorrow mornin,' Arnie," he said at long last.

"Yessir."

"Your kids all right?"

"They're fine. Say, who's this Shem I hear tell about?"

"Hehe, he's got quite the throbs for your Sammie."

"Well doggone, somebody's got to tell me about it."

"He's been helpin' me around the farm. Doin' chores and such."

"Well."

"Don't you warry, son. Shem's a good'n. World ain't gone totally to pot yet."

Just before sunup we rose and entered a forest so cold that I looked behind my shoulder and spotted our vapored breath still curling around tree branches and going up like a priestly offering into the sky. The air had a blueness clinging to it, an undecided light asking for its entrance, still crusted behind new clouds of snow. Trees hung around like shadows in that God-haunted dawn, refractions of a night of heavy stardom; nothing crunched beneath us and I remembered Tate saying the night before that "it's heaven enough." We clutched our rifles and peered through foliage, mystery burdening our backs with broken lightness. It was quiet as all get out. Just a smudge of wind visited the forest and collected a handful of snow, causing it to snake over the ground and catch fire when it escaped the shadows. I could hear Old Tate breathing beside me and noticed him lower his gun. I glanced at him. He was standing knee high in snow with his head set upwards at the frozen boughs. I joined him in the gaze, seeing the pale slate of blue sky, and the branches etched against it. The world was in hibernation. Anything more than a whisper seemed to threaten to wake it all up, and the wind came again, this time a bit stronger and from behind us.

"Strange," whispered Tate. "Sometimes, sonny, when I'm out in mornings like this, it's like I am so close to life. To the pulse of it, you know." I nodded, too reverent to reply yet. He went on, "And moments like these when you know there's more to this vale of tears than meets the eye. Suppose I don't want to go home. Well, suppose there's a better home for me somewhere else? Someplace where the beauty is this doggone astounding every second of every day."

He smiled and faced me. "I almost forgot what we're doin' out here, to be frank with ye, Arnie Tuck."

I nodded. "We were scopin' the woods out for Bigfoot."

"Ah. That's right. Bigfoot. The creature which reflects the country it comes from." Tate narrowed his eyes and chewed the inside of his lip. "And if that critter reflects these woods, then what must he be like?"

I admit I hadn't thought of this afore, but according to standard Bigfoot theory, Bigfoot himself ought to have been as wondrous and beauteous and all-around breath taking as that morning proved to be. So, we stood there in our tracks, dumbfounded, wondering if the guns in our hands were an affront to the glory we were stewing in. It was then that the unexpected happened right before our eyes. We looked on up Scraggly Hill, over which lies my own homestead, on fire from the morning sun, and saw Bigfoot himself hurry up its slope and pause in pure view as if knowing he was being watched. Tate clamped his fingers on my shoulder and suspended his breath. This squatch was something huge, all gristly with brown-red fur, paws like clubs at his sides, and when he turned around, eyes gleaming quite a lovely blue and green down on us. Tate had his buffalo gun, which Lord love him is longer than he is, his wild green eye fixed, body not breathing. I raised up my gun as well, our fingers settled on triggers. Our instincts took over for the moment, and we, for the time being, forgot our former reverie. How I'd kill the brute with a shotgun I didn't know, and I felt pretty stupid pointing it as if to kill, but we didn't end up shooting nothing. The reverie returned. The simmering delight and speechless mercies which possessed old Tate's frozen face told me he had been transfixed by the brute expression came across as an angel's in apelike repose. Bigfoot just peered at us, a little curiously, and doggone it all he *smiled* at us, and then without a word bounded up the rest of the hill, using his hand-paw to up and swing over the edge and gone. It was like we had seen an angel of God, and then the light swarmed the woods with another breath of wind and gave fire to the tear in Tate's bewildered eye. We knew it then by some intuition. We could feel it in our bones. Surely it warn't Bigfoot that was stealing our chicks and goats and all the rest. It couldn't be. The quiet meanderings of those woods prodded a mystery cold and lost and starry, and we lowered the guns and breathed it all in like heaven-heavy pipe smoke.

"Well, I'll be tuck jimmied," Tate whispered. "What a magnificent critter it is. Pardon my soul Lord for wantin' to barrel down one of your sweet Bigfeet. Big old smilin' goon that he is! Big old smilin' goon that I am!"

We had no intention of chasing after the critter. It didn't seem like something you *could* chase. It was the sort of creature that had to come to *you* if you ever wanted to find it. And for some reason it had chosen to be seen by a couple of knuckleheads who, just a day ago, had their hearts on shooting it down only because they didn't know what was swiping their livestock.

So, you see there comes a time when a man's got say "enough is enough" but such a cognition don't mean you'll wind up doing what you thought you would. How could we have shot Bigfoot? All we really wanted to do was take a hike together and get a glimpse of him, deep down, to see the coagulation and locus point of all the beauty and glory and memory of our neck of the woods.

We whooped aloud as the morning broke, snow shimmering in sun as we hiked our way forward above Scraggly Hill where Bigfoot had stood, studying the tracks and punching each other's shoulders at the sight and breathing in all the cold glories which belong to our neck of the woods.

Tate and I trekked on back to my homestead and I'll be darned if I dint see a bobcat slink by the trough and take a gulp and then carry on its merry way into the trees. A stakeout was in order. Heck, maybe there'd be hordes of them come nightfall, an apocalyptic avalanche of cats like the world ain't ever seen, off to steal our chickens whiskey and women, and I muttered the thought to Tate and he said, "'Tis perfectly possibly, sonny. Perfectly possible. We live in a right ornery universe, you know."

Mindy saw us come on down the hill and called to us, "C'mon ye lost sheep! Breakfast is on the table!"

CHAPTER TWO

WELL, it's gone and been a whole week since Old Tate and I wound down the path of destiny and spotted ourselves a real Bigfoot. And if you recall it was quite the holy experience. Seeing that magnificent critter shining in the morning sun, his big old paws hanging at his sides and his big old green eyes staring right into mine. Right special. My boy Bobby asked me about it, wondered if we'd seen anything whilst tramping through the snow, freezing our butts off like dumb jack mules. And I said to him, "Sonny, you go right out yonder into this world and don't let nobody tell you Bigfoot or any other fantastic creature don't exist. 'Cause they do. And there's lots more'n sasquatch to get excited about."

Now Bobby ain't known for his head but for his heart. So he smiled and nodded and said, "Okie doke Poppy!" and I was a right proud pop. Now Mindy, my dear wonderful wife, sweeter than cedar sap on a spring morning, well, let's just go ahead and say she warn't as kin to the idea of me seeing Bigfoot. Claimed whilst she was beating the rug that I'd had one too many the night before with Old Tate and was still seeing shapes accordingly the next morning.

"And now you've gone and spread a whole bunch of hogwash into Bobby, makin' him wanna go out and see a bigfoot like his daddy."

"Mindy darling," I coaxed. "It warn't the whiskey that lent the miracle to my poor eyes. Now c'mon, you gotta believe me here." Splat! She hit the rug with the broom and the dust done exploded in my face. One thing you need to understand is that Mindy is one of those women who'd so much as fight a b'ar to protect her kiddos, but she's a no nonsense kinda lady through n through, and whatever don't need fussing about, well, she opts not to fuss over it. And with all the ghosts and ghouls and Bigfoots afoot in the forest, she thinks that if you leave them alone, they'll return the favor and you can go on tending to your own. So she was right peeved that I'd violated the sacred divide betwixt hillbilly and the unknown. But my question is, why not reconcile with the Bigfeet among us? Heck, mayhaps thar's some other critters out there too just waiting to be discovered: jackalopes and w'arwolves and such, critters that no civilized man has seen or imagined except in their heads. Might as well be a whole another village of such critters just yonder the creek for all we knew.

Without Mindy's knowing I roused a few of the boys along with Old Tate in the barber shop down in Jimmytown, where Charlie give us our trims and then ordered the chairs round the room into a right council-like fashion. I wanted to get everyone's opinion on the goin' ons around these parts and see if they had to advice to offer. It was a bit of a risk, tell you the truth. Some of these buggers don't take too kindly to the unbeknownst. Old Tate set next to me, smoking his pipe and muttering to himself, something about how his poor old back felt like it was about to crack in two. "Dern tractor still won't start," he said. "I'm gonna have to get old Shem to gimme a hand."

"Shem?" I said. "You mean Shem whose got a thing for my sweet Sammie?"

"Hehe, that's the one. I told you not to worry about him, ye old coot. He's a good'n. And a tough worker. That's rare these days."

Joel Wiley asked me if I'd met this new schoolteacher who had just come down from upstate New York, and I said, "No, but Bobby and Sammie tell me he's a real trial come from hell."

"I hear tell he's comin' to the meetin' tonight," Joel said. "That he's goin' to give us a lecture on how there ain't no such thing as Bigfoot."

"I'd ruther die, Joel," I said. "Who's this boy think he is, rompin' in here and lecturin' us? This concerns Bigfoot, tain't two ways about it." By and by, some more of the boys come in and got themselves situated. Tommy wanted a haircut but I told him to wait and grab some coffee, and Old Tate started looking real contemplative about the world, so I didn't bother him again with talk of Shem. The last two fellers to come on in the shop was a short skinny dude dressed in a suit, wearing round glasses and holding three or four books under his arm, looking real impertinent and superior although he warn't no more than five feet tall. And behind him came that hambone Japheth the Fur Trader, all racked up in his coonskins and fox scarves and leather breeches, carrying his rifle and chewing on some deer jerky. His eyebrows were covered in frost and he spat a load of tobacco on the ground so some of it splattered and got on the sophisticated feller's polished shoes. Joel nudged me. "That's the teacher. The spindly one."

"Figures," I said. "What are them volumes he's totin'?"

"Don't matter. Looky there at Japheth." Japheth got himself some coffee and plopped down a few feet away from us.

"I see him."

Everybody in Jimmytown know that Japheth is one proud fool for the books, but he's just about the most committed Bigfoot believer you ever did see, which explained why he popped in for a visit. He wanted that Bigfoot. Wanted that hide spread out on his living room floor for his future kiddos to sprawl on next to the blazing hearth. He'd shot his fair share of the wild. Rabbits, raccoon, bears, field mice. A real champ, that one was. But he was on the verge of craziness looking high and low for Bigfoot. The woman he wants to marry, Mildred Cletus, told he had to bring in the big game if he ever wanted to earn her love—he took that to mean "Bigfoot" and ever since has been out in the wild night and day hunting the critter. He was plumb outraged when he found out that old Tate and I had chanced on the beast first. Plumb peeved if you ask me. Once he heard that Tate and I'd spotted that glorious critter, he went mad looking for tracks in the snow. He was staring at me right then with his beady brown eyes, his unkempt hair all hanging down beneath the coonskin cap. He took another bite of jerky without looking away and I could smell the breath from here.

"Go ahead now," said Tate. "Time's come to start."

I went on ahead and stood up as the room got all quiet, clearing my throat and taking off my beaver hat.

"Thanks all for comin' boys," I said. "Now you all probably got lots of questions and I promise I'll tend to them best I can. But here's the scenario—Tate and I here saw a sasquatch bigger'n the tombs of Timbuktu, on the top of Scraggly Hill near Hogback Creek. Now I know many of y'all are members of the Bigfoot Brethren, so I don't question your faith."

Some of the boys muttered, "Amen," which I thought a tad too zealous, but kept going nonetheless. "But here's the dilemma, see. This warn't no wicked critter set on stealin' our chillun. It was a thing of benevolence, a real angel from above. Now it's my intention to ask all you Bigfoot Brethren to call off the hounds and respect the territory of the sasquatch." Once I said that I noticed Japheth's eyes gleam greedily and his stubbly jawline start working itself. "We ought to extend a hand of friendship to the forest beasts, whatever they end up lookin' like. Anywho. That's my two cents. Tate? You got anything to add?"

Tate stuck out his lower lip and said "no sir-ee" and then went back to his pipe. The teacher in the corner coughed and cleared his throat as I started to sit back down, opening one of the books he was carrying and scoping out some passage with his finger. He seemed real sure of himself but when he talked it sounded like the mewing of a newborn kitten in search of his mommy's teat.

"It is universally decided upon by the National Board of Official Debunkers of Myth that Bigfoot, Sasquatch, or any creature pertaining to the myth of the large ape-like humanoid, does not exist and is a relic of superstitious and uneducated laymen." The prof closed his book and swallowed, tugging at his coat collar and adjusting his spectacles. Now it ought to be said right off the get go that I ain't opposed to a learned man. Heck, learning is what this life is about, if I got anything to say about it. Learning takes a whole lot of courage, the courage to say to yourself, "Maybe I don't know all the ins and outs," and when you can say that, well, you can rest assured that you ain't on no path to folly no more. Been a lot of foolish men who went around preaching all the answers but didn't know dilly squat about loving their wives and mothers and friends, and plenty of folk who couldn't put seven and six together but had a stash of wisdom to the moon and back nonetheless. Anyway, all that to say I didn't much appreciate the tone of this feller and knew right ahead of his speech that he aimed to debunk us all and enlighten our supine little minds. Afore I could say anything, though, Japheth stood up just as he lit a cigarette, so the coals on the end bloomed and ignited that gleam in his eyes again. The poor scholar man backed up against the wall and searched the room for some reassurance.

Japheth didn't say nothing, only puffed at his cigarette and put a hand on his rifle, looking real serious-like. By this time Old Tate was mostly dozed off, pipe nearly falling out of his mouth. "Say, Tate, ye old chigger bite, wake up!" I said.

"So what are ye implyin', mister?" said Joel. "If that book you're readin' is right then what'd the boys see last week? Overgrown field mouse?" We all chuckled.

"I'm assuming it was a large bear, of sorts," said the teacher, whose name I should have already mentioned is Mr. Ham, "and, in the excitement of the hunt, these gentlemen saw something that clearly wasn't there. A Bigfoot." He glanced right at me, swallowed again, and said, "I came to this town to try and teach your children the empirical truth about the world." He talked in a soft voice, like he was trying to prove how humble he was and kept going so our heads were at pains to make sense of the gibberish. "And you know, it was frankly devastating to me how woefully behind in their studies they were. It was my original goal to send one of them to college in New York, even the esteemed college where I was so fortunate to attend. But when I hear these ridiculous rumors about Bigfoot, and you men actually gathering together to discuss this myth's validity, well, it just about ruins my hope for *any* of these kids getting the education they need to get out of here."

Tate frowned suddenly and piped up, "Say, who said anything about them 'getting out'? We're hill folk. We learn what we can and we stick with each other. That's called family, son."

Mr. Ham blushed and pulled on the collar of his suit. "There's a much bigger world outside of Jimmytown, begging your pardon, sir," he said at nearly a whisper. "Cities, institution, governments–"

"Oh the *government* eh?" said Old Man Scooter, who ye could tell was just fuming over there in the opposite corner. Barber Charlie put a hand on his shoulder to calm the man down, and Mr. Ham, well he was just about petrified to the bone by the outburst.

"Don't need no government tellin' us what to do! We get along fine here. Next thing ya know them bulldozers up at Shady Ridge goin' to come down and start expandin' and puttin' in their dang gas stations and parlors and roads and cars, cars, cars, 'til ye can't hear no birds twittering or no river rushin'!"

"All right, Scoot," said Tate, waving a tired hand. "We're all a bit wound up here. Scholar man just tryin' to help, in his own way."

"Maybe that's all we need to talk about now," I added. "Just keep in mind that Bigfoot is out there, but he ain't out to hurt nobody. Not even chickens. Maybe there is somethin' in the woods we ought to take caution of, but it ain't the Sasquatch."

Japheth was the first to leave the shop. He whipped out of there in a huff without saying a word, but I knew he was thinking up a storm. He was thinking of Millie his lover and how he had to please her at all costs—he'd drive himself mad in them snowy woods if he stayed up there for too long. It started to snow again and a cold draft swept into the room, chilling us where we sat. Mr. Ham slipped out next, "shaken and perturbed," as the feller himself might phrase it, and the rest of us mingled a while longer.

"You sure Bigfoot ain't a villain?" Old Man Scooter said, eyeing me with that lazy eye of his.

"If you'd a seen him, you'd understand, Scoot," I said. "Bigfoot's an ally, don't you see? Tate and I, we aimed to shoot that sucker where it stood, but we got a change of heart. What do you reckon that's about? It's Japheth we may need to worry over. He may have some mischief planned and I aim to figure out what." It was still pretty clear that most of the fellers didn't buy my story—they was just too reserved to say so. The standard doctrine amongst the brethren is that Bigfoot exists, sure, but he ain't no cherub on a post, but a real demon-beast which ought not to be tampered with, or else killed off altogether. I feared my speech hadn't convinced the half of them. Tate patted me on the back and we headed on back home.

We parted ways just beneath Moonshine Ridge, and the snow had stopped and up above, a million miles away, the stars spread out and gleamed and it was suddenly all hushed and quiet and still.

Tate's white hair hung back as he craned his neck upwards to check out the view, an old man still shocked at the beauty above his head. His hat tumbled into the snow and I picked it up for him, and he took it chuckling it to himself. "We live in a right ornery universe, Arnie," he said, brushing the snow off his hat. "Right ornery."

Once I's inside I shuffled on over to the wood stove and plunged a couple more logs in there to liven up the flames. The kiddos were both tucked in bed and thar didn't seem to be a soul a' stirring. I checked the big old cuckoo clock Mindy inherited from her pappy and saw that it was near midnight.

I shrugged off the coat and figured I could slip into bed more or less unnoticed, since Mindy she's such a heavy sleeper, see, but as I turned around to draw some water I near fell back into the stove for fright, for there was Mindy glowering at me in her robe, arms crossed and foot tapping the floor.

"Darlin'! You're up awful late."

"Ya think?" she said.

I paused there, backing up too far so my rear got a little roasted by the woodstove, and said, "It's all right honey, I's just out with Old Tate in town, catchin' a smoke." Now this warn't completely untrue, but Mindy can read me like an open map, especially when that map has got a pair of blank eyes and a fumbling tongue and a butt that's nearly in flames.

"You had a meeting about Bigfoot," she said. "Tell me it ain't true."

I decided not to fight back this time, and let my shoulders sag a bit. Shootfire, this woman was good.

"Yes, Mindy," I said. "Just to come clean about what happened last week. And tell the boys that they ought not regard the critter like a kidnapper or thief no more, nor try and hunt his hide, like that derned Japheth."

"I told you once afore, Arnie, that Bigfoot and them other critters and ghouls ain't up for being pals—we ought to stay out of their way, and they'll stay out of ours."

"Well then we're in agreement," I replied. "That's what I's tellin' them—that they ought not mess with the Sasquatch or all the other boogiemen which live out there, perfectly content without our meddlin.'"

"But you want to go off and see Bigfoot again," Mindy went on. "You got that curious gleam in you're eye, the same one ye get when ye smell sarsaparilla and gin. Mighty dangerous trying to explore stuff of the unknown, darlin,' stuff ye don't fully understand. And them Bigfoot mayn't be as generous as you think."

I bunched up my lips and scratched the back of my head at the comment, fuming angry that she'd found me out like she did. She was right, you know. I wanted to chance upon Bigfoot again, and maybe strike up a real connection to the feller, time permitting, but it's like Mindy said—there was lots of stuff I just didn't comprehend, about the woods and its particulars. It was wrong to go out and hunt the squatch, but probably unwise as well to try and repeat our encounter of that glorious beast. We probably couldn't find him again if we tried, so dang elusive them Bigfoot always are. Tate and I had had our miraculous sightseeing. Now it was time to get back to normal and expect nothing more to come from it.

Mindy come up and hugged me and said she loved me, and I told her the same. Then we went on to bed while the woodstove burned long into the night and then died out all the way sometime before dawn.

CHAPTER THREE

T HE next morning, I got up afore the rest of the kin and brewed myself a pot of coffee, revitalizing the wood burning stove and surveying the pink sunrise dabble in the trees and bleed light on the snow. I poured the coffee in a thermos and tramped into the cold. It's a wonder just how quiet it can get out here in the woods. The naked tree branches, black and crooked like statue hands, don't move a whisker in the dawn, and it almost seems as if the whole world is on the inhale breath, preparing for another day of glory and trial, albeit in their right ordinary ways. It's enough to say to yourself, "This ain't just a tree or just a rock or just some snow on the ground. It's all speaking and all so content with itself you figure you could take a lesson and learn to say thanks e'er once in a while." Well, there I am, pontificating again like one of them philosophers, but you know, some sights make you wonder and think good and hard about the bark lines betwixt the timber.

I fed the chickens and collected the eggs and broke the froze water. Our horse, Nimble, came up and nuzzled me, her breath and velvet nose all soft and warm in the sub-zero chill. Looking over her shoulder I glanced at Scraggly Hill, smelling the mystery, my eyes stinging with cold, and imagined the Bigfoot atop it, staring at me with them golden eyes, big hairy hand paws at his side and his legs in the snow up to his knees. And then he's gone, just like that, a figment of the imagination.

Back inside, I set the eggs next to the skillet and Sammie walked on in the room, yawning and spooling out her hair with a comb, still in her nightgown.

"Mornin' sugar plum," I said.

"Morning Daddy. Cold one last night, wasn't it?"

"Supposed to be colder tonight. Get on next to the stove there, and warm yourself."

Sammie curled up next to the fire and I put the eggs on the skillet along with a couple leftover slabs of hogback and let it sizzle to perfection. Sammie said, "Daddy?"

"Uh huh?"

"Well . . . I's just wondering . . . see . . . there's this boy, you know, his name's Shem?" I stopped flipping the egg cold and let the name settle in my psyche. Shem. Tate's helpmeet, apparently—the righteous Shem. Heck, the name's almost as noxious as Japheth, and only a tad more biblical sounding. But for the sake of sweet Sammie, I kept up my composure and went back to stirring hogback. "Shem, I hear tell? Go on."

"Well, he's a real nice boy, see, and he's been working real hard for Mr. Tate Fletcher, since Old Tate's health has been failing so, which is right honorable of him, see." Sammie got up and clutched the edge of the counter, scanning me for signs of displeasure or approval. Personally, all I could do was smell the fat coming off of the hogback, which ain't exactly a divine smell, so now for long as I live when I hear the name "Shem" I'll think of hogback stewing in the frypan. This boy had better be a divine angel himself or I probably wouldn't be able to stand the sight nor smell of him.

"Tate mentioned it," I said, careful not to betray any tone of suspicion.

"Um . . . well, I invited Shem over for supper this evenin'. Ma said it was all right with her, that she'd cook the good steak and mash some taters, and maybe make a chocolate pie afterward. He don't live far. He can make the walk."

I dished out the hogback and eggs and offered some to Sammie, staying silent, realizing that as a father this was one of those moments that don't sit well with the stomach. Makes a man feel like he just got sucker punched, like your pride and joy is bound to eventually get stolen and there ain't nothing you can do about it.

"Sounds fine, honeypot," I said, smiling at her as she nervously took her vittles. I give her the rest of the coffee too—she drinks it black and wouldn't know what to do with one of them cappuccinos they sell in the big city. "Any friend of yours is one of mine." She smiled, her ruddy cheeks glowing with relief and her big green eyes glimmering as the sun overcame the hill and shone through the kitchen. "Thanks Daddy," she said, putting her little hand on mine and sipping some of the coffee. "He's a real nice boy, ye know. He can lift a hundred pounds and he reads poetry sometimes and he knows just about every kind of living thing that crawls on the earth. He don't much like to hunt the critters, but he likes to look at them." I smiled at her, the empty feeling in my stomach turning into something like sorrowful joy, if you understand my meaning, and Mindy appeared in the doorway with little Bobby at her side sucking his thumb. I kissed Mindy on the jaw and introduced them to the hogback and eggs, and we all enjoyed a fine breakfast at the dining room table next to the eastern leaning window.

"Need to gather s'more corn and onions from the barn," I said. "Be right nice sides for dinner tonight." Mindy glanced at me, then at Sammie, who was still looking mighty pleased with herself.

Bobby piped up, "Shem-boy comin' tonight?"

"That's right," said Mindy, wiping the child's grimy face free of hogback. "And you best be on your good behavior, understand?"

"Yes'm."

"When's the chap comin' over?" I inquired, shoveling some more wood in the wood stove and leaning back to light my pipe.

"Six p.m. sharp," said Sammie, eagerly. "He's ridin' his horse over—and I told him we would maybe take the sleigh out for a spin?"

Now I ain't taken the sleigh out for some time, and in fact, generally like to keep the occasions rare. Mindy and I had a fine sleigh ride the eve we were married—we flew over hill and hedge to get to our new cabin I'd just built, Nimble the horse earning her namesake with her chipper leaps through the four feet of new laden snow. And I didn't know exactly why I said, "Why, sure we can, 'tis a good time for it, I wager," or was suddenly so ready to cater to this here Shem's place in our family. Maybe letting go of the notion of seeing Bigfoot again give me a newfound openness to letting things slide, "liberally," as they say. I don't know. All I know is that all this talk of sleighs and dinners and "Shem-boy" sure was making Sammie's darling face beam, and it would be a cruel measure to say no when that countenance is yours for the enjoying.

After the kiddos cleaned up, I went out to the shed and unearthed the old sleigh, the brass blades still in mint condition and the wooden frame still holding its own after so many years. I trussed up Nimble to it and got up in the sleigh and off we went over Scraggly Hill, quick as a squirrel, and into the woods towards Old Tate's place. Hogback Creek was flowing steady, a black vein in a white sheet, and I rode beside its ravine for a spell, with my keen eye surveying the surroundings just to catch a potential glimpse of "you-know-who," and yet knowing that that magical episode is probably passed for good. I slowed Nimble to a stop in a clearing and hopped out, blowing into my hands and taking out my rifle from the back seat of the sleigh, gazing through the scope at the far forest country on the horizon. There warn't no movement, not even of a bird, and the silence went uncut except for that slice of river gurgling somewhere below. But then I spotted something, sure as shoelace. It warn't no buzzard or critter, neither, but a feller draped in all his furs, donned with a coonskin cap and brandishing that shiny Winchester of his. It was young Japheth, the impertinent Bigfoot hunter. He'd probably been out there all night and must've been plumb tuckered out by then, and it showed in his stature. Poor bugger was stooped over and shivering, trudging through the snowdrifts like he was about to plop over and die in one of them. I sighed. That young man had a problem, which ain't no secret, of course. But there's a difference, ye know, in being an honest hunter, and having an obsession that keeps ye awake at night—and all for a gal who wanted a man who could bring in the big game. Lord have mercy, women and their beguiling ways! Sometimes they know beyond the shadow of a doubt that all they got to do is wager a deal with a man and get him to go to all lengths to fulfill his end, and at the end of the day the feller just ends up purely tuckered out for want of some peace of mind. Well, shoot, that makes me a bit sorry for young Japheth, thinking on it like so, and I figured he could at least use a ride on back to his *casa*. Problem was that he was way on the other side of the creek, and the sleigh couldn't manage that kind of acrobatics. So I put my scope away and hollered, "Japheth! Japheth! Get on over and I'll give you a ride!!" I kid ye not, the boy jumped seven feet in the air at the noise and fell over on his rear as a consequence, losing the Winchester in the snow and landing in such a way that his legs were sticking up straight as straw men out of a particularly deep snow drift. To make it worse, a batch of snow came tumbling down from a pine bough above him and buried him where he lay. And doggone it, the fool didn't even *move* after that.

"Well I'll be tuck jimmied if that ain't the darndest boy I ever . . . " I knew then I had to go on over and dig the nimrod out else he might suffocate in there. Leaving the sleigh where it stood, I slid into the ravine, waded in my gaiters across the creek, and scrambled up the other side, hearkening on my younger days for inspiration. Once at the top I hurried over and dug Japheth out of the snow, checking his pulse and other preliminary doings to make sure the goober was still alive. He sputtered and gasped, a bit over dramatically if I's making a judgment, and locked eyes with me.

"TUCK," he breathed. "Arnie TUCK." Japheth needed some serious re-hydration, I wagered. He looked as pitiful as corn pone without the pone. "Ye can't stop me!" he said, struggling like a lamb against its mother ewe. "I intend on skinnin' that squatch and plantin' in right afore my hearth, and I'll be bum jammed if ye think ye aim to protect that monster from me. He's a MONSTER, ye understand, TUCK?"

"You're lovesick and lost," I replied, gently enough, putting my canteen to his lips. "I had an inklin' you'd be fooling round here, figurin' ye might see that glorious critter. But Bigfoot, see, he only shows himself to folk who they KNOW ain't up for shootin' him. Ye'd understand that if ye had half a noggin in your skull."

"How would YOU know, Arnie TUCK? Ye ain't got the copyrights on the ghouls and wizards of the wood." Say what ye will about this ornery kiddo, but he could be right poetic when he wanted to.

"Notwithstanding, I'm just trying to do ye a favor son." By then I was cradling Japheth to the creek and he warn't struggling no more, since by then he was tired as a dog. For a second he felt like a child in my arms, totally infantile, with even a spool of drool turning to ice oozing its way out of his mouth. But I knew that he warn't going to give up easily. It warn't in his nature to give in, and he certainly wanted Millie bad enough. Too much. That gal could have just about any boy in Jimmytown, and she warn't about to compromise her standards for the perfect feller. And Japheth is a looker, no two ways about it, and can cut a tree down with his teeth, and has wrestled more than a few bears to the ground, and coons too, when they nose around the smokehouses.

"Listen, son," I said, shaking him a little just to get my point across. "There are certain things you do for a woman that are honorable—to show her that you're a gentleman and such. But then there are *extremes*, see, when that right desire to please becomes an all consumin' passion—"

"Don't preach to me, Arnie TUCK!" whispered Japheth. "You think this is all about a *girl? Is that what you think?*" Well, to reply privately to myself, yes—that was what we all thought. He must've noticed my confusion and went on panting, "It ain't about Millie. Not no more. See, if I don't catch this here Bigfoot, it means thar's *somethin'* in these woods that's just beyond my reach, that I can't trap nor make a pelt of, and it's that, Arnie TUCK, that makes me so doggone mad outta my *mind!*" It was as if the explanation had roused something fierce in the boy, for he tried to wriggle out of my arms and stand on his feet again, only to take a couple steps forward and plop on back on his face into another snowdrift. I stood up and observed the pathetic feller for a few, wondering if it would serve his sorry rear end to leave him stone cold so he might learn a lesson. But it was awful cold at nights. It was November 28th, and the end of the year has a way of shutting itself up in a freezer. So, I hauled Japheth over my shoulder all the way to the sleigh, and not without some real exertion, and figured that maybe some semblance of mercy would change the poor fool's mind and hopefully show him a road to sanity.

I drove the sleigh all the way to Japheth's cabin, which is about two or three miles away from Hogback, and cradled the boy indoors where I laid him on his bed and stoked a fire in the cold hearth. He didn't have much to eat in there, that was positive. There was some jerky on the table and a kettle of chili, near froze, hanging above the coals of the fire. The walls were littered with his taxidermy—fox, bear, coons and bobcats, and his bed was fairly well made up of hides as well. But there warn't no Bigfoot hide. Until he had that, nothing else would satiate the dweeb. I sighed, tugging some furs over the boy's head and shutting the door behind me as I left. I learned later that it warn't long at all before Japheth was back out in the woods on his quest for glory, and this time I probably wouldn't chance on him in time afore he ruined himself.

Back at the house, everyone was up in arms over supper, with Sammie stirring and mashing and rolling, flour on her face and her eyes dead set on her objectives—honey ham, taters, cream corn, and green beans. "Yiiippp!" I said, stamping my feet at the door. "Sho does smell MIGHTY fine in here!"

"Uh-huh," said Mindy, shaking up a bottle of rum so her hips swayed. "And Sammie here is doin' just about all the work herself. I'm a right proud Mama."

I almost wondered aloud if this here Shem was worth all the hullabaloo but bit my tongue and went ahead and shoveled my boots off. "Say, where's Bobby?" I asked.

"Oh, buildin' a snow fort I reckon. He's supposed to be workin' on his arithmetic, but it's a Saturday, after all—can't talk no sense into the boy."

"He oughta be in here helping too. I'll fetch him."

The afternoon passed. Bobby came in and out of the house, and we did our part in cleaning up the parlor and arranging things to a tee. Then we all calmed down for a spell later in the afternoon, and Bobby curled up on my lap in front of the woodstove, then went off again to score some new mischief. As I was sitting there all pensive-like, I got to thinking on Shem again, and started feeling a strange impulse to get all authoritative and cold-like to the young sonny, like he had to cross certain dots to gain my approval. Was it right? I don't know. When it's your daughter, you have to think it to be at least reasonable. Too many fellers come around trying to court gals and succeed in buttering up the fam, just to go on a break her heart later. You hear those stories and it makes a father wonder. There are boys out there like Japheth—wolves in wolves clothing, and there are boys out there you never suspect—wolves in *sheep's* clothing, like the Lord warned us.

Folks like that ain't especially concerned with treating others with charity and respect. Rather, they aim to get on the inside of things and cause violence to the whole edifice, if you gather my meaning. Japheth, now he was a feller who couldn't stand not having power over Bigfoot. That was the real explanation for his wild escapades in the woods. He hated the very idea of there being something beyond his manipulation. Again, I don't know. I can only trust the right man will come along for Sammie and pray to the good Lord that my Bobby gets raised up to *be* the right man for that special lady.

Well, enough philosophizing. The table was set, and the candles were lit, and it was up to me to keep a lookout through the window to see if our long-anticipated guest was alighting over the hill. Sammie had put herself in her blue frilly dress and done her hair up so she looked like a young copy of her Mama, except all herself and unique too, and the sight nearly brought me to tears. Bobby had to be coerced into his Sunday suit and didn't look so anticipatory. As I peered through the curtain, I saw the head of a horse appear over the hill and the figure of a feller atop it, holding a lantern at his side and wearing a broad-brimmed hat.

"Somebody's here," I said. "Maybe it's the mailman. Hehe!"

"Oh Daddy, stop it!" cried Sammie, joining me at the window. "It's him! It's Shem."

"Shem-boy!" Bobby cooed.

Shem tied his horse up at the post in the front yard and could be seen slicking his hair back nervously. He warn't no swaggering cowboy, that was for sure, but he sure did look round and squat out there in the dusk. The sky was clear and pale purple, carving out the trees against itself.

"All right—dinner's all set and Shem's here. All is as planned."

The boy knocked on the door and Mindy opened it up with a bright smile and cocked head, and in came the culprit, Shem Tellingsworth, holding his hat tightly and exploring the room and its inhabitants like a scared coyote. He was dressed in his Sunday suit, all pressed and spotless, and looked first at Mindy with a soft, "Howdy do, ma'am," then at Sammie with a sharp inhale of atmosphere and a trembly smile, and then at me—and the smile and the color in his ruddy round face plumb vanished. His eyes got big and blank and he looked about like he was hyperventilating something awful to the point I felt right sorry for the young buck. "Sir," he said, extending a hand, which I shook firm and hard. "M-my name is Shem T-tellingsworth and I—I am right pleased to me you, sir—and it's been a real honor gettin' to know Sammie, sir, and, uh, well, dinner looks wonderful!" I slapped him on the arm and said, "Proud to meet you, Shemmy. Set down and eat! You had a long ride over?"

"Oh, no sir. Not long. I live right near close to Old Tate, where I been doin' some work."

"Fine, fine."

Shem fingered the edge of his hat and shuffled a bit closer to Sammie, who, beaming and blushing like sunshine, gave a little "curtsy" and said, "Welcome, Shem!" Bobby gaped at the ordeal like he was watching a motion picture while Shem took her little hand and, as if he warn't so sure what to do with it, gave it a quick peck with his lips, after which he nearly swooned with embarrassment and clutched the mantelpiece for support.

"Hey now!" I chortled. "Now that we're all acquainted for the evenin', let's eat, shorn't we?"

Shem gave an artificial chuckle in response and set himself down next to Sammie, whilst I took my place at the head of the table and Mindy set opposite with Bobby in his little chair next to her. "Sweet thing," said Mindy, "will you say the grace for the meal?"

We all bowed our heads and clasped hands, so I let the silence settle for a second or two, then prayed, "Dear Lord Jesus, we thankee verily for the bounties of your blessings, for the snow and the woods and the wild—for this family and this home. And we thankee fer bringin' us this here Shem . . . " Here the boy slightly cleared his throat. " . . . and pray for his wellbeing and health in all things. In your name, I pray, amen and amen!"

Everyone echoed the "amen" and Mindy went to serving everybody up a fair share of ham, taters, cream corn, and green beans, and Sammie excused herself for a bit to fetch the oat rolls too. Shem observed the other plates, sometimes clearing his bangs out of his eyes and biting his lip, and when we all had the continents arranged on the platters, he waited for me to set into the ham, and then politely nibbled on his mashed taters.

The table was quiet for the first bit of the dinner, as I well expected. It takes a while when a newcomer is present just to get adjusted, you understand. The meal was spectacular, and there was enough for everyone to have three or four portions. One thing we believe on Scraggly Hill and Jimmytown at large: food's for eating, no two ways about it, and the more the merrier. You ought to have been here on Thanksgiving. Heck, just about the whole county came down for the feast, including some of them city folk from Shady Ridge, but it warn't no thing—the centrality of a feast is that it's open table, and ain't nobody gets less than anybody else, unless they're being ornery about their portions.

Eventually Mindy broke the ice and asked Shem how his mama, Jemimah, was doing.

"Oh, she's fine, thank you,'" said Shem, soft as a newborn lamb. He swallowed a strand of green bean and managed the courage to add, "She's expectin' again, in fact."

Mindy set down her fork and let her shoulders drop, showing her disbelief. "Jemimah! Pregnant again! Well, I'll be. Ain't that wonderful! You're gonna have a little guy or gal for a pal pretty soon, ain't that right?"

Shem smiled, nodded, and said, "Yes'm, we're right excited. She's doin' well, and Pa is workin' on buildin' a new crib out in the wood shop." He seemed to gain some confidence at this juncture, adding, "And we're goin' to paint it either blue or pink based on if it's a boy or girl that comes out, and I'm workin' on carvin' some figurines to hang from the ceilin' so the babe can look at them from the crib."

"That's wonderful, Shem," said Sammie, softly.

"Yes." He glanced at me, then went quiet again and returned to his ham. Was I scowling at the boy, scaring him off? No, because Mindy warn't giving me "the eye" and I felt that my smiling muscles were all but spent with use. Turned out the kid was just plain nervous, wanting to give off a good impression, but it was such that he was pining away with the efforts of it all. Now I respect an honest plea to honor your elders in the community but comes a time when that "fear of man" starts to control your every move if you let it, and I do reckon Shem was under its sway that very moment. I thought back to earlier that day when I wondered if I should act all cold and stern to the feller, but now I was tempted to break out the guitar and accordion and do some jigs just to cheer him up!

"Well, Shem!" I said, and realized a second after that I should've waited for him to finish his swallow of water, for my outburst caused him to snort it out his nose all over his plate.

"Oh dear!" said Sammie. "Daddy, you ought not shout at the table like that!"

"Sorry, sonny," I said, much more softly. "Didn't mean to shock you. Here." We all offered our napkins to mop up the melee, and as soon as Shem reached equilibrium again he said, "Yes, sir. Sorry sir. You were sayin'?"

"Oh! Well. I's just wonderin' what kinda work you been doin' over at Tate's. He's old as Methuselah and no doubt needs all the help he can get. Ha!"

Shem swallowed and proceeded with caution. "Yes sir. Ha. Well, uh . . . I been workin' on his tractor quite a bit, and shovellin' snow every mornin' since the weather don't seem to be relentin', and I go ice fishin' for him from time to bring in a trout or two. And I'm still trampin' around the woods lookin' for his missin' goats."

"Missin' goats, eh? More missin'?"

"Yes sir. There ain't wind nor tail of them. I can't find a carcass, nor tracks. Can't expect to find tracks, I suppose, given how much it's been snowin' lately. But still. It's an odd . . . ordeal."

"We never did exactly figure out just what was snatchin' our farm animals," I said, stroking my chin and furrowing my brow. Shem stared expectantly at me, frozen in place by the way I seemed to be contemplating so. Now Mindy perked up and squinted her eyes at me, wondering if I's gonna bring up "you know who."

Bobby was the first to spill the beans, crying out, "Was it Bigfoot, Daddy?"

Shem glanced at Bobby and smiled, turning back to me as I thoughtfully chewed a bit of ham and lifted a fork in a gesture of speculative response.

"Bigfoot . . . if he even exists, mind ye, don't want no trouble with poor farmer folk like us and Old Man Tate. There's got to be another explanation." Shem nodded in agreement.

"A mystery," said Sammie with a sigh. "You ought to have a stakeout, Daddy. See if it's been foxes, or bobcats, or coyotes. Surely it's somethin' else."

"That's right. Just because we don't know *what* is doin' the stealin' don't mean we have to blame Bigfoot. Can't blame what we can't understand simply to make ourselves feel better." I paused, and the table was silent, and I went to thinking about what I'd said, and if I was contemplative before, I was *real* contemplative now.

Later that eve, we all piled into the sleigh, and Nimble set off through the snow under a silvery full moon. Shem and Sammie were huddled together in the back, a mite too close together, I wagered, but what have ye, with Bobby up against Sammie and Mindy pressed up next to me. I guided the sleigh along the main road that hit Jimmytown, where the lights and lanterns were faintly glimmering in the darkness like stars in the sky, except they were yellow against a quilt of white. We got into town and was met with some howdy dos from some folks at the cafe who were handing out hot chocolates to young'uns in the street. I pulled the sleigh up next to them after everyone submitted their orders for the hot chocolate and found that it was Old Man Scooter and his wife Becky giving the goods out.

"Howdy, Arnie," said Scoot, handing the kiddos their hot chocolates and pouring me my own cup of jo. "Mindy! A cold one tonight. I see ye brought out the sleigh."

"Yep. Brought it out of the mothballs to take the fam for a ride." Scooter saw Shem and gave me a grin, and I punched him in the arm. "A new addition to bunch, eh, Tuck? Hehehe."

"Sammie's got enough suitors to suit her for some time," I rebutted under my breath, returning the grin.

"How's business?" asked Mindy.

"Oh, same as always, I suppose. That new teacher feller, Mr. Ham," said Becky, stamping her little feet in the snow. "He's been comin' in most mornings and suppin' on coffee and chocolate pudding. He loves chocolate puddin', now don't he, darlin'? Always readin' over his books."

"Well, he's probably doubling your business, then!" I said.

"He ain't gaining no weight, that's certain," said Scooter. "Still as spindly as ever."

"Where is he from again?" asked Mindy, looking full of motherly concern. "That poor boy. All the way out here at the coldest time of the year, and ain't married? No family connection?"

"Apparently, he's the second cousin of Cedar Billyboot, and come down per Cedar's request. You know Cedar," said Scooter, shrugging. "Always trying to help his own, even if they are New York city folks."

"New York," Mindy said to herself. "Well, I'll be."

"He come down to teach since Mrs. Fergie passed to glory, as ye know," said Becky. "They warn't about to approve it at town council, seeing they didn't know the feller, but they didn't have no other choice but to hire him, for everyone else in Jimmytown seemed otherwise occupied." We all knew this, but in Jimmytown, big goings-on always got repeated around hundred times or so until something new come along to rattle everyone's chains.

"That makes sense," said Mindy.

"He lives right around the corner, in fact," muttered Scooter, pointing in his leather gloves. "He stays in a flat above the auditorium, by the mercies of Mr. Searcey."

"Say, Arnie," said Scoot, changing the topic. "You hear the rumors?"

"What rumors?"

"That's it been Bigfoot that's stealing all these here critters and gear and whatnot."

"Who told you that?"

"Japheth come by this morning and said he saw Bigfoot swipe his own mule. Said he found tracks. Tracks bigger than any man's." Scooter sighed, shrugged his shoulders. "I don't know. He's a crafty one, that Japheth, and wants his share of glory too intensely, if you ask me."

"Amen," I muttered. "It ain't no thing, Scoot, I can tell ye that much. Something else is swiping our critters. I just know it."

"Warn't only the mule," added Scooter. "Tate's goats. Your chickens. Cats and dogs that used to roam the Jimmytown streets ain't been seen fer a month . . . Jerome's pet squirrel is missing, and that thing's more faithful that a hound dog!"

"It's a mystery," Mindy put in. "What ought we do about it, do ye think?"

"It's time for a stakeout," I said. "A real bona fide stakeout. Maybe I'll take Shem with me. Shem and Old Tate."

At the mention of his name, Shem deposited a bit of his cocoa from mouth to sidewalk, as if he'd been summoned to the guillotine, and warily looked our way, afeard of what we were going to say next.

"Be good for the feller," said Scooter, slapping the boy's arm. "You got a rifle of your own, son?"

Shem swallowed, and replied, "Well, no, not exactly. I got a .22 pistol, but it ain't really nothing to sneeze at."

"He's a stupendous shot," Sammie interjected.

"A pistol would do, I reckon," said Scooter. Shem returned forlornly to his hot chocolate whilst Sammie tried to cheer him up again, telling him he wouldn't have to shoot nothing, but just strap a pistol to himself to look the part. That Shem was a particular character—I recanted my previous ideas of breaking down the boy's "pride." Now it appeared the buckaroo needed precisely the opposite! Some folks don't need humbling the same way kings and tyrants do. Some folks, the Shems of the world, need to be shown that they got *courage,* doggone it, and just need to have it tested for it to show! Studying Shem and the way he opened the door of the sleigh for Sammie and used his tiny kerchief to wipe the hot chocolate off the lap of her blouse and reddened like a Christmas plum every time she laughed at one of his sayings, I figured the chap would make a right honorable gentleman if he just had the chance to do good in a situation of real consequence. I stroked my chin and nodded to myself, and Mindy looked all suspicious, with her hands on her hips, like she knew exactly what I's thinking (which, Lord love her, she probably did), and off we went back home, through the star laden woods. "It's been a wonderful night!" Sammie laughed.

As we proceeded back home, I heard an owl go *hoo hoo* somewhere off in the tall sycamores, and when I looked down up to the clean face of Scraggly Hill, I spotted a gray fox prance into the untouched snow, buried to his chest, and then pause in place to cast a pair of glittery green eyes straight into mine. My heart felt a thrill for some reason, and the stars seemed to shine all the brighter at the contact, but before I knew it, the critter was gone, leaving its paw prints in place and nothing but a silver moon to shed light on them.

CHAPTER FOUR

I T was all in the papers over the next week or so. We staked out, Shem, Tate, Scooter, and I, but saw nothing but a lost poodle, and nearly froze our butts off sitting there in the snow. It all came to nil. Whatever was stealing our critters was real stealthy, that was for sure. And what was in the papers, you ask? The news of the same sort of thievery happening over in Shady Ridge, that's what. But it warn't just critters that was going missing. No sir. Apparently, it was all manner of things: tractors, automobiles, even rifles and guns, and food. Apparently also some folks were saying that they saw "a big hunched figure" romping through the woods on numerous occasions, and his eyes were gold like fire in the night, though he made no sound, and prowess and power and terror of the forest was his name.

It fetched a load of introspection for me, I'll tell ye that much. I ain't one for ruminating on something I can't control directly, since what's the p'int in it? But this here was a dilemma that for some reason kept rending my poor heart through the midsection. I laid awake at night, and I think Mindy was awake too by the way she was breathing. But I didn't say nothing, not sure what it was I wanted to speak of. It's a strange thing when there's a thief in the woods and yet ye can't find the source, and that puts a germ of fear in folks, if ye understand—a dose of uncertainty is what the devils give to prime us up for the Fall, and we more often than not gulp it straight down without a second thought. For if ye don't know what's threatening ye, the first thing we tend to lash out against is the unknown, the *otherness,* as they say, and right now that *other* was the Bigfoot. Didn't matter that Tate and I had laid eyes on him and reported of his friendly glories. Didn't matter if they'd see the beast themselves, for a miracle of sight can't teach the soul to trust. So, I tossed and turned about every night for a few days, until on one of them Mindy laid a hand on my shoulder and whispered, "Arnie? You all right?"

I sat up in bed, her hand on my back, and looked out the window, up into the stars that gave just a tint of light to the skeletal trees below.

"I don't know, honey," I said. "The rumors in town and all about Bigfoot being the thief. Well." I looked down on her where she lay, her deep brown eyes half closed but awake and attentive. She was listening, all right. I could always count on that. "Do you believe them?"

She raised herself on an elbow. "I don't know snuff about Bigfoot," she whispered. "But I believe *you.* That's what I signed up for, when I married you. To trust you. Rain snow or shine."

I smiled, bending over and kissing her long and tender. "I can't explain it," I said, still bent low near her. "If you could have seen that critter, Mindy . . . was like I saw a king . . . so free. So itself. It was like . . . like it was one with itself and the hill, with the snow and the trees and the birds . . . ah. I sound like a fool."

She smiled, nodded. "I'm sorry I wasn't pleased at your interest in the sasquatch, darlin'. It's just that . . . well. I don't know. I guess it's just hard to tell what's good and bad in the world beyond the hill. On the other side of the creek."

"I know. I know."

"But you don't have to worry about that now. I'm here. We're all here."

And I slept all right from then there on out.

The next Monday it was "take your daddy to school day," which comes annual, and since I'd gotten curious of Mr. Ham and his ideologies and ponderings, I decided to go on over and set in on a class or two. Sammie was in one classroom with the older kids, whilst Bobby was in the nursery with Mrs. Tellingsworth—Shem's mama, she was. I come in to find that there warn't no other daddies present, which I's surprised by, since I like to think that the elders of Jimmytown want to know what sort of stuff is being pried into their offspring. Sammie sat down at her bench near the window, and Shem nervously took a seat a couple desks away from her, but warn't nobody else going to sit between them. So I did! I plopped down betwixt the lovebirds and clapped Shem on the shoulder, and Sammie crooned, "Daddy, be gentler on him!" and pretty soon Mr. Ham come in the classroom through a backdoor which presumably led to his study.

He was well dressed and dignified looking like ever he was, with his round glasses perched on the edge of his nose and his black hair slicked over to one side. He was a nervous fellow, but sophisticated as they come, and I don't believe there was a time when he was up there teaching that he didn't have some classic of literature or philosophy tucked under his arm, though he never cracked it open to read from it. Turns out I'd come in on that morning's class called "naturalism," which apparently is supposed to be on all things natural. Sounded all right to me, so I kicked back for the lecture whilst the other children mournfully opened their textbooks. Heck, they seemed to be at a funeral, so forlorn they seemed to me. Sammie sighed and Shem stared blankly at the page in front of him as if mentally preparing for the tortuous agony they was all about to be put through. It was dead quiet. Not a sound nor peep from nobody. Mr. Ham noticed me there, and seemed to swallow at the sight, then smiled and nodded, and started to address the class with a dead pan voice to which only a mortified zombie comes close to competing with. I'll try to translate best as I 'member how.

"Good morning, class. As you know, this is a class in which I . . . and only I . . . will speak. I will take your questions at the VERY end of today's three hour, in depth lecture." I heard a slight whimper behind me, probably from Little Andy, who ain't known for his calm and patient learning habits. Mr. Ham swallowed again and turned to the board, drawing a little squiggly thing with the chalk and then pointing and saying, "You remember last week's lesson, don't you? How our ancient ancestors were all one primordial goo with no brains or bodies, and then over time they became fishes in the ocean, and then leaped up on earth to become apes, which over time transpired into intelligent human animals?" Everyone nodded slow and sad, as was becoming of the topic, I realized.

"Excellent. New discoveries in the fields of biology and archaeology have affirmed the mere animality of man, and all categories pertaining thereof, and along with said discoveries and findings, the old ways of making sense of the world . . . " Here the feller glanced a bit warily in my direction but had the gumption to keep going, "Such as myths, religions, 'metanarratives' and the like, simply don't have their place in society anymore."

At this Little Andy raised a hand and said, "Say Mr. Ham, by myths don't ye mean ghouls and ghosts and spirits and such? Why, those is real as rainbows! Ain't ye ever seen a ghoul, Mr. Ham?"

"What did I say about asking questions, student?" said Mr. Ham. Poor Andy let his hand fall back on the table and mumbled, "None taken 'til the end of class."

"That's right. Now the question I'm going to be asking all of you is how do we live robust and powerful lives when we've been given the knowledge of our origins, which, as mentioned last week and again this morning, were little less than a thimble sized drop of goop as stupid as a rock?" The room, as you might imagine, was *quiet* as a rock after this question, which to me seemed to have the plainest answer in the world. I didn't say it, but Sammie and Shem could both tell that I's starting to get unsettled. My knee began to pulse and I felt the urge to twist the ends of my beard. "That is the question every modern man must ask himself. He must rest his chin in his hand and stare morosely into the window of his soul, only to realize that he *doesn't* have a soul, that the sages of all the great religions were wrong to believe in truth outside the five senses—and then he must ask himself, 'How then shall I live?' You see, little citizens, if you do not see the truth that, in the grand scheme of things, you are, in essence, that spot of accidental goop at the bottom of the ocean, you will continue to abide by these comforting myths and lies that your . . . ancestors have passed down to you." Well that done made me near livid, I do declare. It took the restraining of the Holy Ghost to keep me sane in my seat, but Lordy I was having a time with this Mr. Ham. What's that he was jawing of? That we was nothing more than primordial ooze? Heck, everyone knows that nature changes. That's sure as shoelace. But dumb old ooze? It was an insult, I wagered, an absolute insult of an idea. "So the idea that there is anything at all 'spiritual' or 'mythical' out there in the woods, like boogeyman or Bigfoot, has been totally disproved, young scholars of humanity." Mr. Ham went on like this for some time, talking about the particulars of certain discoveries and whatnot, saying how the universe come up out of nothing like a magic spell put it there, except it wasn't done by magic. The man droned on until I and the rest of the students were nearly dead with despair. And THEN, just when I thought it couldn't get no worse, Mr. Ham goes, "All right, NOW it's time to study Humanitarianism, students. I know, I know . . . this stuff about you basically being a cog in a great ruthless machine can be disheartening, but now we come to brighter subjects: the capacity of human beings to create the ideal societies they want to live in. Take a city like New York City, where I came from. It's a beacon of human achievement. The buildings, the museums, the art and architecture, the parks, the coffee houses, the auditoriums." Mr. Ham sighed, looking starry eyed and smiling, as if it was his unfortunate fate to have had to leave that shining beacon of human achievement and teach its glories to hillbilly fools like us. I personally don't take much stock in cities. The noise and busyness and weeping and the shouting and the demonic rush of automobiles and bikers and taxi drivers with no compass, moral or physical—makes a man want to retreat deep into the woods and smoke a long one in Old Tate's cabin over a glass of moonshine. If the spirits of the world take the shape as ghouls and ghosts in our neck of the woods, they take the form of a business suit and dollar sign over yonder. And people say there ain't no spirits!

"We can create meaning for ourselves if we attain enough knowledge and education of arts and culture and all things glorious and sophisticated," Ham went on. "We come to realize that since we're just here for a few years and then we die and no one remembers us unless we do something great and wonderful, that we need to craft great and enduring civilizations, for although man *is* nothing more than a cog in a machine, for reason or another he still wants to be remembered forever. And so, students, what do you have? Rome. The Parthenon. London. The Chinese Dynasties. Politics and press rooms. New York City."

I's trying to follow Mr. Ham's line of reasoning. Truly I was. We ain't no more than goop. Got that much. But now we ought to go achieve glory? What kinda glory? A delusion and a dream, that's what, and I wanted to say as much. But afore I could, the bell rang at long last, and the kids let out a sigh of relief, running out the door in streams while Mr. Ham chimed out their reading assignment. "Read pages 80-118, and remember, your fifteen-page paper on all of this material is due THIS Friday!" I went out with Sammie and Shem, scratching the back of my head and in a fair state of dire straits, to be quite candid with ye. No wonder my poor kids kept groaning to no end over school, feeling like the very souls in them were being squelched and oppressed.

"That does it," I said.

"What do you mean, Daddy?" said Sammy.

"I aim to find Bigfoot and bring him to town, and show that sorry feller what fer. And if that don't work, well I pray the good Lord would strike him with a miracle and a proper heart, for he ain't got a *speck* of sense, that professor."

Then a thought struck me. It occurred to me that all of Mr. Ham's theories would be fairly torn to shreds if he laid eyes on a real creature of spiritual import, such as Bigfoot. If I went from a feller eager to gun Bigfoot down, why wouldn't the cynical skeptic become a genuine believe if he were given the chance? So, it was decided. I aimed to find Bigfoot and wager with him about making himself known and famous to Mr. Ham, and Japheth too, along with Mindy and all the other cautionary types. Then they'd know what *I* knew, that sense of real glory, of holy heaven on earth. Then they wouldn't be so lusty or doubtful or afraid. Little did I know that trying to harness what you ought to leave alone, or rather trying to lasso the glory that's meant to lasso *you*, will generally always land ye in a hole in the ground with nary a hand to help you out of it.

CHAPTER FIVE

THE next morning, I went looking for tracks to see what I could find, still in a fit from the day before. I walked a long way without seeing tracks. Not even deer tracks. The white canvas went unperturbed, keeping the woods sound asleep in its drapery. There warn't no birds a-tweeting then, nor wind rustling the tree branches. 'Twas all quiet and blue and white, the trees gray and black and frozen to their spindly cores. I felt righteous in the quest. Like I was on a mission to save the town from lies about Bigfoot, and how were they to believe that he was a good old boy and not a thief or a legend? By seeing him for themselves, that's how. There warn't no other way except to present the facts to them plain as day. You noticed, probably, that I didn't invite Old Tate to come along with me, and that ought to tell you a thing or two. He wouldn't have nothing of it, I figured. He'd say to me, "Arnie, ye got a heart of gold but you're tryna place your butt in business in which there ain't no butts allowed! We chanced upon Bigfoot, and he smiled on us and give us something to ponder but trying to bring him in to prove a point ain't going to bode well for ye, sonny." Yep, I knew exactly what the old wise man would have said but I went right into the wilderness notwithstanding, in the impertinence and hurry of a child sniffing for candy. Lordy, like that fool Japheth . . .

While I was tramping along so confidently, I got a sliver of motion in my periphery and stopped cold, leveling my gun up to my eyes and peering through the sites. Nothing. Then, I saw it again, just a blur of motion, and it looked like something small—a bunny rabbit nearly, and yet with some extra bulk on it that I couldn't quite pinpoint. I stepped forward, lowering the gun, noticing something like a tree branch sticking ever so slightly from behind a big oak tree. And then, the critter done showed itself, stepping out from its hiding place and blinking at me with a pair of beady black eyes. And I be tuck jimmied and flung if it warn't a full-fledged jackalope, wearing a little blue military coat with silver buttons and a blunderbuss strapped to its back, its head of antlers stretching a couple feet above its furry brown head, its snowshoe feet cradling its whole body in the snow. It had a paw on the blunderbuss and squinted at me, then, as if realizing who I was, straightened and give me a salute, saying in a chipper voice, "The Colonel at your service, good sir! You wouldn't happen to be Arnie Tuck, would you?

I was dumbstruck, tell you the truth, and didn't quite know how to respond to the little beast, for I ain't never heard a critter talk before. Bark and yowl and mew? You bet. But speak plain English like a regular citizen? Not in a million years.

"Blub..boo," I said, though I meant to say something like "howdy do?" The "Colonel," as he called himself, lowered his salute and fingered his chin, like he was examining some Neanderthal in a museum.

"He told me you human beings could talk," he said. "Hmm. Perhaps he was . . . ahem . . . misinformed?"

I didn't understand who "he" was nor what this jackalope's particular vocation might be, but by the looks of him he looked about ready to call the cavalry to arms and ride to battle against an army seven times the size of his own. He had that confident air about him, like he was ready to conquer the world and tear down tyrants and demi-lords by the dozens.

"No. You ain't misinformed," I said. "I'm human. And I can talk. What's your business, Colonel? You'll excuse me.I ain't never heard a critter like you talk afore. Heck, ain't never seen the likes of a jackalope afore either!"

"But you've seen something better," said the Colonel. "You saw Bigfoot. The best of us all. Our shining leader. Our visionary. Our King!" He must've been moved in passion by his spiel, for the jackalope dropped to one knee and laid a paw on his chest in reverence, then stood back up wiping a tear from his cheek.

"You saw Bigfoot—in all his glory. He knew you were out to get him. But he also knew you were an okay guy, Arnie."

"You know the Sasquatch?" I said.

"It is my esteemed honor to serve in Bigfoot's administration as his eminent Colonel," said the jackalope, putting the paw back on his chest, except this time closing the eyes and lifting his chin to look dignified and supreme, though by golly he warn't no more than two foot tall, I wagered. "But my countenance darkens, Arnie Tuck," the Colonel went on, frowning. "There's trouble in the woods. You know about in some detail."

"Our farm animals been gettin' snatched, it's true," I said. "We aim to have a stakeout tonight, in fact, tryin' to figger out what's swipin' the poor devils."

"Hmm. A tragedy in the first order, Mr. Tuck," the Colonel whispered, shaking his head and scratching an antler. "We've had our suspicions of a suspect. Actually we're pretty sure we know who precisely has been committing all these misdeeds."

"*You* know?" I said. "Well, there's a lot to discover in these wild woods, that much is clear!"

"Oh Mr. Tuck!" cried the impassioned beast. "If only you could remain in the bliss of ignorance! Come with me." The Colonel took the blunderbuss in his paws and hopped daintily through the snow, casting a glance here and there to make sure I's following close behind. Sometimes the Colonel would freeze in his tracks and point the gun afore him, then chuckle to himself and mutter, "Just a broken twig. Can't be TOO careful around here." He made it seem like we were trespassing through a dangerous war zone of sorts, and had to keep our heads down to stay out the line of fire. He kept looking every which way, tiptoeing through the snow to stay quiet, sniffing the winter air, usually just to comment on the type of bark we were passing by.

"A sweet elm. Post oak. Ahh . . . a little blue spruce!"

His vigilance and environmental conscientiousness had me both a bit concerned and amused, like I was following a half soldier and half tour guide.

"Spies everywhere," he whispered. "Absolutely everywhere. Hiding in the snow. Pretending to be branches on a tree! Still as stumps in the woods. Can't be too careful." The Colonel breathed in deeply, then exhaled, shaking his head and muttering some words that I couldn't quite understand.

"You'll understand that I have a couple questions, Colonel," I said, quietly as a I could. "Who are the spies? Spyin' on what?"

"We can't talk here, Arnie," said the Colonel, apologetically. "Not safe. Nowhere is safe in these dark times, mind ye. But not here. We're in a red zone." I had a mind to ask what was "red zone," but figured I'd get the same response, so kept quiet as we continued. It was well on into the morning at that point, and the forest life had perked up a bit. Squirrels flitted up and down the trees, and birds cooed and chirped amongst each other above us. Suddenly black crow cawed at us from an ominous perch in a tall sycamore, causing the Colonel to cry, "Dip and dive, soldier!" and leap behind the nearest tree. I followed suit best I could, hiding behind a mess of briars and trying to comprehend what the fuss was all about. The crow took flight and swooped low to the ground, cawing and aiming his head towards us, then flew up above the trees and went soaring southwards.

"Great Scot," breathed the Colonel. "That was a spy of the enemy if I ever DID see one."

"What, that crow?" I said, laughing and rising to my feet. "Weren't nothin' but a crow, if ye don't mind me giving my own two cents."

The Colonel brushed himself off and cocked the blunderbuss as if for extra effect, stared me down with his beady eyes, and said serious as a stone, "It wasn't just a crow, Arnie Tuck. Lesson number one of the woods. DON'T assume every critter is a pal. 'Specially those that aren't a member of the Creature Kingdom."

"Creature Kingdom?"

"Ye heard me correctly." The Colonel took out a carrot from his military purse and chomped down on its end. "Carrot?" he said, offering me the other half. I politely abstained. "So crows ain't part of the kingdom?"

"Oh there's plenty of crows in the kingdom," the Colonel said. "I know many a good'n me-self, in fact. But friendly crows generally don't *caw* at ye at first sight. A Kingdom crow might gently flutter down to a lower branch and say somethin' like, 'Well, hey there, Colonel, what's the rub?' and I'd say somethin' like, 'Not much, just huntin' down rebels and wanna-be tyrants is all,' and the crow would thus respond, 'Hey! I'll keep an eye for ye with my bird eye, how's that?' and I'd go, 'That's right honorable of ye, crow bird! Please do report to his eminence or myself if ye find ANY suspicious activity.' And then the crow would off and fly and bid me 'fine one' and THEN he would go cawin', then and ONLY then."

"Ah, I see. Grateful fer the explanation." We went a bit farther, so we reached a shallow part of Hogback Creek where the water ran broad and shallow over a bed of blue stones. The Colonel stopped at its banks and bent low on his four paws to take a drink, then crossed his arms as if pondering an important question. "Here we come to the great border, partin' the portions," mused the Jackalope.

"How's that?" I said.

He turned around and said, "Behind you is hillbilly country. Your country. You didn't know that? On t'other side, well, that's the Creature Kingdom."

"I warn't aware there was a divide betwixt us," I said. "But I s'pose Old Tate and I was on the other side of the creek the morn we spotted Bigfoot."

"You were trespassin'," the Colonel said. "But we talked it over at the Gathering of Critters Tall & Small and decided that though ye may have meant harm to the king ye didn't go through with it. To the contrary, by all accounts it seems to have proved to be a right transformative experience for ye!"

"That it was," I replied, kneeling down and dipping my palm into the icy cold water for a drink. "We thought it was him that was stealin' the goats and chickens, but, I can't explain it, Colonel." I shook my head, wiped my beard dry from water, though not afore some it froze at the end. "It warn't no ordinary Bigfoot. Can't figure it. But just the sight of the critter made it plain that we'd stumbled into holy territory, if ye gather my meanin.'"

"That I do. And that's why we pardoned ye and the ancient old man. If ye'd shot Bigfoot, on the other hand, well, let's just the Hogback Creek might've been breached by some Creature Kingdom emissaries lookin' for some righteous recompense for the deed."

"I see. Shootfire."

"But see there's a rogue on the loose, and that calls for a border crossin.' Since it concerns you and your village, I could use your help. These are dark days."

"Sure thing, Colonel. But one thing. Who's this rogue?"

"Ah. There's a cohort, no doubt, but it's led by—hey, watch out!!"

A snowball the size of a basketball barreled its way from across the river, pummeling the poor Colonel where he stood and shooting him backwards into a frozen grove of wheat grass. My Lord. It was an ambush. Some group of devils up on the opposite ridge was hurtling down snowballs and stones by the dozens, so by the time I could crawl for cover I had been duly peppered with artillery.

"Colonel!" I called. "Colonel! Are you all right?" Still the assault rained over our heads, but I couldn't get a view of the attackers. They must've set up some barracks up on the ridge and could aim with such precision that their little heads and paws went entirely undetected. By and by the Colonel roused himself from the snow, a wild red gleam suddenly burning in his eyes, and leaped upon a low-hanging branch with the blunderbuss cocked and aimed.

"So it begins, Arnie Tuck!" the critter hollered in a blood curdling voice. "Don't think. Just shoot!"

And shoot he did, lemme tell you. Don't ask me what in the sam hill was proceeding outta that blunderbuss, but it was something cooked up in the heart of Hades. To my human point of view, the missiles looked like snowballs wreathed in some kinda blue fire, but who knows what it really was. All I know is that it was causing real havoc to the other side, and some real remorse amongst the enemy cohort. BOOM! BOOM! BOOM! Went the blunderbuss, over and over. BOOM—KAPOW! BOOM—KA-POW! A shot fired and an explosion resulted, like measured clockwork. The jackalope was on something of a warpath, hollering and yipping like a sore hound dog, and I do declare that I hardly even fired a shot I's so enamored by him, his cock and aim and pull of the gun, his eyes suddenly gone red with fury, his big old footpaws twitching, all agitated with righteous rage.

"For the Creature Kingdom!" came his war cry once the onslaught of snowballs against us dwindled and died out completely. But he didn't take no rest at the end of it. No sir.

"Hurry!" he yelled, slinging the blunderbuss over his shoulder again and leaping down from the tree. "Pursue! Pursue the fiends!" I didn't know what we were pursuing or for what righteous cause, but next thing I know we had tramped through the creek and scrambling up the other snowbank. "They won't get far, the rebel fools!" the Colonel hissed, clawing snow and soil. "The cowards always flee! But this time they shan't have no safe resort nor refuge! AYYYEEEE!!!"

The Colonel reached the top of the snowbank well afore I did, and by the time I crawled to level ground, huffing and puffing like a dog, he was already bounding away after a scattered group of—was I seeing straight? Yep. They were bobcats, wearing red capes and running like the dickens for cover.

"Well, I'll be barbecued," I whispered to myself. "It was bobcats the whole time."

CHAPTER SIX

W E chased the bobcat legion across Crater's Field and into another copse of trees, known as Bobblehead Woods because the trees are so spindly and "bobble" like figurine heads. There they all climbed up in the branches and peered down at us with their yeller little eyes, mewing and hissing as the Colonel came to a stop to give them heck. "You'll pay for your crimes, rebels!" he shouted, shaking a paw.

"Easy now, Colonel," one of the bobcats replied. He might've been the chief of the herd, since he was the biggest, and the most raggedy looking, with notched ears and a mangy arm. He let some drool fall from his mouth so the Colonel had to dodge it where it landed, and added, "You've underestimated our numbers. Mew mew!" (That was a bobcat laugh, if ye were wondering.) "And our leader gains power every day! Forging new alliances, crafting new schemes, mapping more territory! He will never rest until all the county lies under the power of his paw." The cat glanced at me and went, "Phht phht!"

"You've brought a human with you," he said, standing up on the narrow tree branch and bending forward for a closer look. "Ah yes. The chicken farmer! The lowly little chicken farmer."

"Ye've been stealin' my chickens. You and your motley crew!" I said, gripping my rifle and lifting it ever so slightly. The bobcat narrowed its eyes at the gesture and I could see his stump of a tail shaking somethin' fierce.

"Hissss, phhtt phhtt! You hill folk are always so *uppity*. Thinking that you own the forest, the creeks, the fields! No more!" The bobcat extended a paw towards his panting colleagues. "The age of the bobcat has arrived! Bigfoot and his usurpation have crumbled. Now is the time. For revolution! For revolt! For justice! For--" It was clear that the Colonel warn't having none of this nonsense, for he'd aimed his blunderbuss upward and let a snowball fly with such speed and precision that I didn't even *see* the unfortunate target until he was crumpled in a heap at the foot of the tree.

"He ain't dead," said the Colonel as the other bobcats gnashed their fangs at us. "Just anesthetized." The Colonel knelt down to check the poor bugger's pulse, and I stood close behind, surveying the cats above me as they shook the snowdrifts off their branches.

"He'll come round in a few hours," the Colonel decided. "The other traitors will limp back to their masters in due time. Meanwhile--" I wish I could say the good Colonel could finish his sentence, but alas, it warn't so. There was a war whoop that thundered all around us, and suddenly the whole danged forest was teeming with bobcats, armed squirrels, weasels, even black bears and little forest gnomes that smelled like spilled spaghetti. Shootfire, there was a mess of them, and they all come out from the snow and behind trees and amongst the bushes, perfectly camouflaged like they'd been doggone waiting on us.

"Hands up!" demanded a bobcat just a few feet to my right. "Lay the gun down, mister." He spoke in a nasally voice, like he got a toad stuck midway down his throat and hadn't quite graduated from puberty yet, but he looked a tough customer, that's certain, all burly and furry and puffed up. His eyes were a sparkly green, gleaming in the sunshine, but they had a wicked bent to them, like they was grasping after something they just couldn't get ahold of. What was peculiar about this particular cat was his teeth—the two front incisors were big and triangular, like a vampire's, and the tips of his ears were curly and pointy, taller than your average bobcat's. Plus, he wore a purple cape with a silver symbol of a cat eye on it.

The Colonel growled underneath his breath, "Meet Duke Deauchamp Domchomp the 17th. Or Dew Dommy Doo Doo for short."

"That's a mouthful," I whispered.

"Silence, fools!" mewed the duke, strutting forth in his princely manner and sniffing at my knees, which were well buried in snow. "You smell of chicken and hog hoof," he said. Lordy, what a day. First a talking jackalope and now a bobcat who turned out to be spoiled royalty, and with an army of rebel critters at his heels! What next? Turns out, there was loads more wilder than that, and what turned out to be an innocent enough morning of searching for tracks turned into something mighty ominous. This didn't look so good for me nor the Colonel. The rebel army itself looked fairly bloodthirsty, like they's on a mission to start history from ground zero, "upset the established order," as they say.

Dew Dommy Doo Doo knelt next to his fallen chief at the foot of the tree and gave a horrid yowl at the Colonel, stripping him of the blunderbuss and hissing, "You felled a valiant soldier. You led a human into Creature Kingdom territory. You are trespassing into the holy Duke's domain. Your antlers are not properly polished. There are at least sixteen major code violations that I currently detect in your present demeanor. What's the penalty for all these felonies?"

"The brig of doom! The brig of doom!" the army chanted. "Put him in the brig of doom!"

"And what of the human?" the Duke laughed, snatching my rifle plum out of my hands and doing some kind of somersault over my head, whopping my cheek and swiping my beaver hat off in the process.

"Put him there too! Put him there too!"

"Oh ho! Prisoners of war, eh! Haha! *Now* we're talking." Then it got all the more comical and devilish. This here uppity bobcat got up on his hind legs and put his paws on his hips and started to *waltz* about whilst the whole army gazed on and cheered him. The Duke sung out:

The war is good,
The war is great ,
Now it's time,
To enjoy our fate!

Enemies be cursed,
Enemies by danged,
Let them slobber and burst,
and let them be maimed!

No time for fools,
Nor kooks or dumb beasts,
It's time for the common critter,
To be in charge of the big feasts!

All's welcome aboard
So long as ye worship me,
But yer dead if ye decide
To remain stalwart and "free."

We're startin' over,
No more old and bland.
Time to build our babel,
And we need EVERY hand!!

When the li'l fool sung the last line, the whole chorus joined in with a rabid cheer, and clashed their weaponry together and cried out, "Ayee yoop!" and it was just about the darndest tomfoolery a man ever did lay eyes on.

"Fear not, Arnie," the Colonel whispered. "King Bigfoot has resources yet to free us from the entanglements of our enemies. This is not the end!"

I sure hoped he was right. It feels awful strange to be taken prisoner by critters of which are less than half your size but are ten times as pompous. Duke Deuchamp Domchomp was there jigging in the snow whilst some squirrels blasted their miniature trumpets, and the noise and clanging and ruckus got to making my ears ring for pain.

"All right, enough of that!" said the duke as the trumpets petered out. "Time to tend to the wounded and cast these foes into the throes of justice. You know what to do, Skeevy Squirrel Squad (or S.S.S. for short).

"Aye aye, Dew Dommy!" chattered a gray squirrel wearing and eye patch and a pistol at his hip. "Okay boys. Tie them up!" And I do declare that was when the two of us were taken into official custody of the wicked duke, and it would take a work of Providence to get us out. And now for the recounting of the March to Creaky Forest.

There are some things which ain't written in textbooks. Some stuff ain't written there because folks aim not to recall certain aspects of the past. Not so wise a judgment, if ye ask me, but to err is human and there warn't nobody which didn't stretch the facts here and there. But some things, some places, well—they just off the map entirely, see, and don't exactly come under the public eye. Some sights your average hillbilly ain't even seen. And let me say this: the Creaky Forest is one of them. I'd heard rumors of the place, sure. My own pappy, when he was alive, told me and my brothers and sisters all about legends of the Forest, how a witch ghoul haunted it, and when creatures went in, they's put under a spell so they come out looking disfigured. Ye know, all the child-friendly stuff ye tell your kiddos just so they got a proper sense of boundaries. I took a whole lot of stock in those tales when I was just a boy, and crossed my heart and hoped to die that I wouldn't never go near no Creaky Forest, even if my very life depended on it. But as time goes by, sometimes ye forget those enchanted stories. They lessen in their potency, if ye read me. But golly my Lord, the stories come back around with a vengeance that day we were captured by the rebels, for they took the "road less traveled" right towards the Creaky Forest itself. It was a spindly, crusty trail which led to it, where the snow was fine as dust and whipped all around so ye could see the ground beneath. I felt a bayonet nudge me along, and the Colonel was tight jawed, and we were all quiet as we headed towards the entry, where the trees became extra gnarled and bare, all sooty and knotted with age and death. Vultures perched on the branches and looked down with red eyes, and the place smelled stale, of burnt leaves and bad water. I didn't like the looks of the forest one bit and knew why my old man was so keen on getting it into my head how this wood was bent on bad magic. But I supposed it was where these buggers were laying low, growing some army to score who knows what kind of mischief.

The Colonel kept his cool well enough. If we talked to one another, we got a swift kick from the behind, usually from a squirrel, which meant that the blow warn't too damaging, but their li'l bayonets felt like a needle in my back so I stayed quiet. We got into the forest itself by and by, and the air got considerable darker, and the whole place was hushed, laden with old leaves and dry webs and crusty Spanish moss. I heard no water running nor wind a' blowing. It was as if time herself had gone to the outhouse and plumb forgot to come back. There were crows gawking at us and mangy critters of unknown origin slinking to and fro in the thorny shadows.

"Here we are, scurvy!" said the Duke. I didn't know whether he was talking to me and the Colonel or his rebel cohort, but whichever way it warn't much of a welcome. The trail wound on, 'til the raggedy crew led us to a tree so thick and squat that it almost looked like a house without no sense of dimension. It was all covered in bumps and warts and knots, and the branches was all crooked and bare. Stowed away in a big old hole right above a round door in the tree sat a huge vulture with a chain round its neck, who come on out of hiding and peered down on us with these awful eyes, and I do declare the sight of it done sent the bejeebies down my spine. It gave a nod to the Duke, who come up short of the tree and said, "Morpheus, I have a couple of prisoners for you. Wicked ones these are—contrary to the goals of the Duke and the Ghoul." Now when he said the "Ghoul" I done got another sinister shiver down my spine and wondered if the Colonel and I had met our doom in this here woodling.

Morpheus, I s'pose he was called, fumbled with chain around his neck until he come up with a big black key at its end, and then flapped down to the door and opened her up.

"Listen here, Dew Dommy," hissed the Colonel as we was led forward. "You may think you've won, but see here, there's good and beauty left in Creature Kingdom yet, and lots more critters willin' to raze this wicked wood to the ground, ya hear?" The Duke didn't say nothing, but looked ahead with a stoic stare so nary a whisker on him twitched. The Colonel added as we was getting pushed through the dastardly door and inside the tree, "You was a good one once, Duke. The best, in fact. Don't you 'member? How you used to dance so good at the Bigfoot banquets, with all t'other bob kitties throwin' daisies at your feet? 'Member how you played that banjo so swell?" I'll be tuck jimmied if I didn't see at least the inkling of a tear in that proud bobcat's eye at the Colonel's entreaty, and the twitch of a whisker too. But still he didn't say a word. "You can come back, Dommy! The king'll forgive you, paws down. 'Tain't no thing to admit ye made a mistake . . . c'mon now!"

"Put them in Cell 60, jailer!" the bobcat wheezed. "And don't let them see no light of day, neither!" With that the door shut behind us and the vulture prodded us down a spiral staircase that looked like it stretched a thousand miles down.

The vulture critter led us, still tied up, past all these cells bored into the earth, within which we couldn't see nary a thing moving, but it seemed like they was being used, locked tight as they was. I shuddered. Who knew this horrible place existed? 'Twas like Hades on earth, my land! I got to thinking of Mindy, and Sammie and Bobby, and Old Tate, and how the lot of them must be worried by now of my whereabouts. Warn't no matter—I'd find my way out all right, Lord willing. Plus, I had the Colonel with me. Surely he'd hatch up a handsome plan and we'd be outta there in a jiffy and a squeeze. But Lordy, it was a long, long way down those stairs.

At long last we got to the bottom of the spiral staircase and ended up in a small, damp chamber with just the one torch glimmering on a stand next to an open cell door. Afore we knew it the two of us was in the "brig of doom" and the door was shut and locked, and off the vulture brooded with its wings lifted ever so slightly above the naked head. And then it was all quiet.

The Colonel plopped down on the bench and grabbed his antlers with his paws and said, "Awww heck fire, Arnie. This is all my doin,' it is. If ye hadn't chanced upon my cowardly hide then you'd be with your family, roastin' mutton on the fire or some such divine luxury!"

"There now, don't talk nonsense, young buck," I said. "We're in a pinch but it'll turn out all right. Just you wait." I wrung the iron bars to test their strength and couldn't budge them an inch, and then set down aside the Colonel, stroking my beard and realizing how much it smelled like old onions down there.

"Well, I'm to blame for chasin' those hooligan cats into the wood. I was—dare I say—*overconfident!*"

"Ye were the picture of valor," I said, but it was clear the critter wouldn't take the solace. He was a warrior, and his pride and dignity were wounded through the floor, lower than the brig even. He laid his antlers against the wall and gently cried so his furry shoulders throbbed, so all I could do was lay my hand on his back and say, "Shh, now . . . when my Bobby gets a little pouty I always say, 'Now Bobby, whatcha on about? Don't ye know life's too short to snort and sneeze over it? Come now, sonny, look on up! Stars and sun and sky are there even if clouds obscure them.'" At that the Colonel was quiet for a moment, then wiped his beady eyes and leaned back against my shoulder. "Thankee," he whispered. "It ain't the way of the King's Colonel to lose hope so quick. Well, I suppose we'll have to dream of them stars tonight, to tide us over." We warn't comfortable, but was tuckered out to the degree that we drifted off to sleep right nicely after a few minutes, me against the wall and the jackalope against my arm. And dream of stars and free spaces we did, all the way 'til morning.

CHAPTER SEVEN

T HERE warn't no telling whether it was day or night down in that dungeon. The torch flickered by help of some kind of stinky oil, and when we was asleep a bowl of water and a scrap of bread were left in the cell. The hours seemed to just roll right on by. At first, I told myself and the Colonel that would be well, that somebody or another would come to our rescue afore long. And yet the longer we waited, getting hungrier by the minute, all boxed up in that cell, the more agitated I got, wondering if in fact all *was* going to be well. Funny how quick a man's false optimism runs out in times of trial. When life's going pat fine, it's easy to chortle over life's blessings, but when you're in what the Good Book calls "sheol," well, tain't so easy. The Colonel and I talked every now and again. Turns out he was married to a beautiful black squirrel named Zambadine, and they lived in a "nest-house" somewhere in the woods near Dragon's Lake. "It's hard balancing my war duties with family life," the Colonel admitted. "The Detective and I are sent on so many missions, see. It's dangerous business, and we don't never see the end of it. But it's a rich, beauteous life, it is." The "Detective" he went on about was apparently a gray fox that hardly every let himself be seen by the public eye. I thought back to the other night when I saw a fox leap across the hill in the snow, and wondered if that might've been him.

"Our hoot owls serve as sentinels, but the crows of the enemy are just as numerous," sighed the Colonel.

"Now that's one thing I'm a bit confused by," I said. "The Duke—he serves somebody else, don't he? Somebody bigger?"

The poor jackalope raised his head and stared at me head on with those mournful eyes and glumly nodded.

"Oh yes. Ye probably know the tales of the ghoul and ghost order."

"And the w'arwolves, and witches, and all the foulness that fouls up the world so," I added. The Colonel nodded. "They all answer to one Ghoul. He's the source of it all. 'Nameless' they call him, because even the Ghoul himself has forgotten what he was called, and don't see a p'int in names anyway, for he likens folks and critters to *things,* and *things* ain't got names." That made me shiver. "Ain't nobody seen the Ghoul in Creature Kingdom in a long time, but his raggedy old followers slip through our owl posts every now and then to tempt and swipe a good one from the vine." He sighed again. "That's what happened to the Duke, except it was his own fault, in the end. When Bigfoot was crowned King at the Festival of Carrat-nook, when all the population was there for the sight, somethin' went sour in him as we watched that crown descend . . . his heart darkened, maybe, and he was simply eaten up with the jealousy of the throne. And that warn't like Dew Dommy back in his youth. Heck fire, the bob kitty used to play the organ at the Critter Chapel on Sunday mornings and sing 'Leanin' on the E'erlasting Arms' better than anyone in the congregation, I declare! So he's spoiled goods, I guess ye could say. Slunk off to see what the Ghoul had to offer."

"And the Ghoul *did* have somethin' to offer?" I asked.

"That's how he reels critters in," said the Colonel. "Promises them somethin' good and shiny. Like a part of the forest once it's captured. The Duke had access to every corner of the Creature Kingdom under the tutelage of the King. The lake, the woods, the creek, et cetera. He was a champion of a climber, he was, and loved to clamber up them sycamore trees and wave in the wind and watch the stars. I used to go with him. We were friends, the Duke and I, when we was little folk. Raised near each other, we were. He nearly saved my life once too, when a wild boar came ragin' after me over by Moonskunk Barrow. But when he got up into the Royal Courts and Internal Creature Affairs, well, he warn't so partial about the woods nor the creek no more. Nor our friendship." Another long, pitiable sigh from the furry contemplative. "He went the government route, and I the path of the soldier. He chose royalty and I chose the blunderbuss. We couldn't've strayed more far apart during those years of service to the Creature Kingdom, but we both had a common love for the boundaries of the kingdom, and we didn't want to see it go under. Why would we? It was our home. Surely we'd spend our snuff dyin' to save her dignity. But even the noblest of souls can get caught up in its own nobility, and I think that's what happened to the bub. He was promised the crown of Creature Kingdom, if he could do what he was told by the Ghoul."

"That's a real shame," I said, and meant it, too.

"Yes. It's a slow but subtle thing—the workings of power in a critter's mind. When ye think ye need somethin' that really ye don't, and told that if ye don't get it then ye've been duped and short changed, well then it's a quick plunge down into chaos and sorrow, it is, and often takes a miracle to escape it. That's what happened to the Duke. Plain and simple. And it could happen to any of us, ye know. Ain't none of us beyond the grasp of the wiles of the Ghoul, or from our own wily hearts for that matter either."

"So the Duke. He's the one stealin' all the animals and tractors and bulldozers and such."

"Oh no, Arnie." The Colonel leaned up close to me, brows furrowed, and said, "One of *your* folks has been doin' that."

I felt my stomach lurch. "Japheth!" I said.

At this point in this rambling tale of mine, an explanation may be in due order. Ye may want to know that while the Colonel and I were rotting away in that brig there was much ado about something in Jimmytown. If what's reported to me is correct, something like the following happened in a flurry: First off, Mindy started calling neighbors to see if they'd seen me around, and of course, they all said no, they hadn't seen me since preaching on

Sunday. Old Tate was down with a cold and fever and Shem was tending to him, but when he heard I was missing, he got up and headed for the door! But Shem apparently reasoned it out of him and got him a whiskey and that was lights out for Old Tate. Mr. Ham got wind of the incident the next morning in class, and could hardly get the kids' attention together since they was all whispering about whether Bigfoot had captured me. The consensus at the time was that, yes, Bigfoot had stolen me away for causing trouble and 'et me up quicker than you can say "Zap." In a way, there was truth to that understanding. I blamed myself for the situation I's in, for it was my own anger and impatience which compelled me out into the woods without forethought. Like I said, Tate wouldn't have allowed it if he'd a' known. I was striving to clamp onto something which was meant to be left alone, to be disclosed in its own time. Anywho, Mr. Ham assured the kiddos time and again that it "most certainly" wasn't Bigfoot that "kidnapped the good farmer and domesticator of chicken and guinea fowl." Instead, it was probable that I'd simply gotten lost in a blizzard and failed to find my way back, but surely I'd show up eventually. That put Sammie over the edge. She yelled, "That's a load of hogwash! My daddy knows these woods better than any man in Jimmytown—I bet you'd last a full ten seconds outside city limits—for he is right: ye ain't got a LICK of sense, Mr. Ham!" And out she stormed, with Shem following sheepishly behind her. A day passed. The Colonel and I were getting wore out down there in the brig. Meanwhile, Japheth came into town on his mule and called together the Bigfoot Brethren, stirring them all up by calling out, "This don't take no thought. It's as clear as day. First the chickens. Then the goats. Then the tractors and guns. Only natural that the folks themselves should start getting snatched. What's next? Our wives? Our children? Granted I ain't got neither but YOU boys do! I'm callin' for a Bigfoot hunt. If ALL of us join up, that wicked squatch ain't got a chance."

"Aye aye!" they all shouted. "Time to put an end to it, once and for all!" Never mind that I'd personally reiterated to these fellers that they should never suspect Bigfoot for even stealing a daisy from a windowsill. Once I was gone, that was the last straw.

Who else was there to blame? It was off to cross Hogback Creek to storm the sacred keep of things unknown, but that sneaky Japheth, per usual, had another plan hatched up his pantaloons. He claimed that he'd seen Bigfoot the night before stealing away a hat full of eggs from Miss Shrivers' hen house, and had followed the tracks to Bobblehead Wood where was "doggone certain" Bigfoot was setting up camp. So they all snatched their guns, pistols, and grubbing hoes and set off that very night, crossing the creek and clambering up into the Creature Kingdom territory with Japheth at the helm of the march. Old Man Scooter was following at the back, thinking twice about all this hullabaloo, and wondering if there warn't a whole another ordeal going on entirely which no one had considered. Well, he had the right hunch. Once they got to Bobblehead, Japheth stopped and looked around, and it was dead quiet by then. Not a hoot owl nor crow's caw to be heard. "Well?" called out Ed Loom, the shoemaker. "Ye said he was here, didn't ye? Wh'ar in the sam hill is he?" Japheth put a finger to his mouth and squinted into the darkness. The torches flickered, the stars blazed overhead, and pretty soon the sound of their breathing became a burdensome noise. The men shuffled where they stood, feeling the cold against their sweaty brows. Old Tate warn't there to guide them back to common sense. If he was, he would've told everybody to stop acting like they was scared coyotes and go on back home to think on a better plan.

Japheth took a step forward, hands clamped on his shiny Winchester, his coonskin cap lazily donned on his head, eyes glinting for a sight in the forest. He was waiting. Then it happened. In one motion, Duke Domchamp Deuchamp and his wretched army swung forth out of the trees and from among the bushes and started giving the boys heckfire. Little arrows and rocks pelted them where they stood, and by and by the whole company got snatched up in the air by a mesh trap, whilst Japheth slunk behind a tree and watched it all unfold. The boys barely knew what'd happened, but it became clear in a jiffy.

"Traitor!" screamed Old Man Scooter. "It was YOU! You're the one in league with devilry!" They was all struggling to break free from their bonds but the mesh was made of cedar root, which don't go breaking in a hurry. The Duke come up next to Japheth and said, "Well done. You've lived up to your promise. All the able bodied fellers of Jimmytown at our disposal . . . and *you are now the new mayor.*" So that was the bugger's motivation. He was in league with the Duke and Ghoul to compromise Jimmytown just so he could claim some measly authority. If that don't beat all.

"You promised me Bigfoot too, when all was said and done," said Japheth. The Duke chuckled. "Oh yes. The 'King.' Do you think I carry him in my back pocket? His hiddenness is his most obvious and damnable trait! He's not static royalty, sitting in a throne all day. Oh no. He's on the move. Always giving glimpses of himself to critters who he thinks could use it. The impertinence! That's why when I rule the Creature Kingdom—that is—at the discretion of the Mighty Ghoul, of course. I will make everyone pay homage to *me,* like a *real* king does."

"I want the squatch's hide on my floor," Japheth went on as a platoon of squirrels shot sleeping darts into the net that was thrashing around so violent. "I don't care who kills it."

"We'll see about that, young Japheth. Now come. Time to take these fools to the camp, where they will be enlisted for mandatory military service in the Ghoul's Gambit ." Now that all the men was sedated and snoring loud as a locomotive, they lowered down the trap and drug them off like a wolf lugging its prey to the den of the beast.

But little did they know that, though all the big, bold men of Jimmytown were sleeping like babes in the hands of a dastardly enemy, that a young, timid hillbilly boy had followed at a distance carrying nothing but a .22 pistol in his mitted hands. He was on his horse, which he unsaddled and tied to a tree on hillbilly soil, and danced over the rocks of the creek until he was standing in the field, alone, and unsure of what to do next. He saw the men get ram-shackled and stolen away in the night, and also the crows and weasels "standing" guard at the helm of Bobblehead Wood. "Those fools will lose their heads and follow the fur trader," Old Tate had told him. "I fear trouble's waitin' on them. Ye can't speak sense into a man when he's impassioned, prejudiced against the unknown. So go another way. Follow your gut, kid. Ye've got spirit, and a courage ye don't yet understand. For if ye got love for somethin' or someone, why, ye'll summon the courage to protect it." It was after those words were spoken that young Shem Tellingsworth tramped out into the snow with one plain objective in his head: "I've got to find Sammie's daddy, and by golly I won't quit until I do."

He crouched in place for a spell, eyeing the forest, heart thundering at the fact that a load of townsfolk had just been carted away by bobcats, but given the strangeness of all the forest legends, he warn't *too* surprised. So he started skirting Bobblehead Wood alongside the creek, staying in the shadows, wading through snowdrifts with the pistol clenched in his hand all the while. Ye might be wondering, *Was he scared?* Well certainly he was scared! He didn't know where he was going, or if he was going to succeed at his goal at that, but he knew he needed to act, and that nobody else was going to do it for him. But see, it ain't the lack of fear which makes a man strong, but his ability to act strongly even when he's afeard. That's the virtue called courage, and it's a right honorable one—in fact, if ye ain't got courage then I'd have to wonder if ye have *any* of the old virtues.

Shem made it past the wood and, covered in shadows, knelt low to the ground to see a trail of footprints leading off to the south. By light of the stars and moon he noticed a small object that looked to have been trampled underfoot, and bending close, saw that it was a small handkerchief with the initials A.T. etched in golden thread the top. Mindy had sewn that into the kerchief when we was first married, and I always had it in my back pocket, but it must've fallen out when the Colonel and I were kidnapped. And thank the good Lord that it did! Now Shem had some direction to off of. He quickly started off after the tracks, quiet as he could, and by and by come up to the Creaky Forest, where the snow went dry like dust and the wind uncovered the thin, black trail leading into its wretched heart. Here, the young Shem stopped in his tracks and stared at the sight. He must've smelt the cold rot and rusty potency of the trees, the metallic taste of wind on his parched tongue, and felt the strange weight of a burdensome task on his shoulders all at once.

It must have been right around then that I must tell you that I felt the bane of discouragement weighing on my own shoulders, making me wonder if we was ever to get out of this stinky old tree. I got to thinking of how painfully worried sick Mindy would be, how distraught the kids, and what about Old Tate? Good Lord knows he might kick the can any day. But the image which kept on rectifying my morbid thinking come as a revelation just as much as it was memory, and that was the face and smile of Bigfoot himself. I know! Don't ask me to explain it. But it was as if that the face was saying, "'Tis all right, ye old coot. There're deeper, stronger truths than the bitter roots of the Creaky Forest—ye just ain't inclined to notice them at your darkest hour." Comes a time in every man's life when he's got to say to himself "enough is enough" and despite all the woes of the world, go on hoping anyway.

The Colonel and I hadn't been fed for three or four meals and took turns taking naps on the bench while the other sat against the wall and counted sheep in his head. The Colonel slept better than me because of his size, so I was purely tuckered out afore too long. My thoughts wandered, and I said a little prayer, holding on to the memories of home and hearth and the touch and laugh of Mindy. I was about to fall asleep, immersed in the thoughts, when I thought I heard a scuffle at the top of the spiral staircase. The Colonel heard it too, for he was wide awake in an instance with a paw at his side as if trying to draw a sword. "Did you hear that?" he whispered. "A siege, perhaps?" We didn't know what it was. But soon we heard a gunshot rattle the silence and a thump of something dead fall on the ground, and then the quick patter of steps getting louder every second. The Colonel and I clasped the iron bars, waiting. Still the sound grew. Who could it be? Friend or foe? After a minute or two, the suspect revealed himself in the dimly lit chamber, obscure at first, but then ever clearer once he picked up the torch from the wall and held it heroically above his head. Lord love him. It was young Shem!

"Mr. Tuck!" he cried, leaping forth with the vulture's key in his hand.

"I'll be blasted. Shemmy my boy! What are you doing in these cursed parts of the world?"

"I'm here to save you, sir, and your friend." The Colonel bowed and introduced himself with an attending salute.

"We have to hurry," Shem said as the doors flung wide. "Someone was bound to hear the shot." Honestly, I was still marveling at the dad gummed bravery of this kiddo. And the same one who could hardly make eye contact a week earlier! Strange, this pliant thing we call human nature. What did I tell you? I *knew* someone would come through for us!

"Good sir," said the Colonel as Shem steadied me. "You didn't happen to set eyes on a radiant blunderbuss with the golden etchings *The Wrath of Sidney Rosco* on the side, did you?"

"Afraid not, Colonel," said Shem. "Your kidnappers must've taken it away."

"Then they will be sorry."

"I can't tell ye how glad I am to see you son," I said, weakly gripping the boy's shoulder.

"Don't thank me yet, Mr. Tuck. I ain't succeeded yet." We started up the spiral staircase, listening keenly for suspicious noises, and as we passed by the other cell doors, we noticed shriveled pairs of paws extending through the bars, and voices going, "Help me!" The other prisoners! They was in there after all. "Does that key work for all of these?" I wondered aloud, and Shem stuck it in the cell's keyhole to figure it out. By golly it worked easy as could be, and out limped a little red fox who looked as if he ain't seen the daylight in decades. "Thankee kindly," he whispered, bowing his head to Shem. "A human. Interesting! We gave up hope of ever getting rescued." The fox went on to explain how he'd been canned for an absurd charge of crossing Jellyjam Basin after sundown, even though he's been a nocturnal son of a gun ever since he was a pup. "The Duke's a hard ruler," he said. "Got no heart except to please the Ghoul."

On up we went, freeing long bound critters left and right. There was a host of black squirrels, some coyotes, bobcats, crows, and tree gnomes that look like dark roots come to life, except with green and gold robes draped on them. It was enough to form a coalition, and warn't a one of them interested in letting the Duke get away with his crimes. At the doorway, I saw the vulture shot dead by Shem's bullet, and then turned around and told everyone to hush. Then the Colonel said, "All right, gentles and lady-critters, I know it must feel good to finally be free, but we're still in the dead center of Creaky Forest, we mustn't forget, and it's bound to be a time getting out of here unnoticed."

I should also mention that there was a fair amount of ghouls that come out of the Old Prisoner's Tree. They warn't so disagreeable. Apparently, there are good ghouls and foul ones too, but they tend to be a bit "thinned" of ordinary substance and talk in whispers, and generally wear pale sheets for clothes. They also float around and can pass through solid things, and like to tell the living to enjoy their beloveds in the present moment, for when the time's past, there's no going back. A ghoul ain't really "there," see. You can see him, but he's lost texture to the point where there's barely half a presence to commune with. But still the few of them trailed behind us, curious of our next action.

"I saw the Duke kidnap some of Jimmytown's strongest and finest fellers," said Shem, after swallowing. 'Twas likely that he warn't too used to rallying a group of forest critters. "We could really use some extra hands to get them back, safe and sound."

"It's askin' a lot," I added. But the Colonel shook his antlers at us and raised his arms high as if readying to call on the Muses for aid, then declared, "Will we desist in this dark hour, when our own brethren most dearly need us? Nay! C'mon, ye weak and weary, if ye have the strength. Time to storm the Ghoul's Gambit. Time to let justice rain down on Creature Kingdom!" With that, the whole cohort erupted in cheers and hollers. Bears stomped their paws, root gnomes clapped their tendrils, and the bobcats shouted out, "Down with the Duke! He betrayed those of his own fur!" They couldn't be held back after that. They broke the door down and started galloping through the Creaky Forest as if hell was on their heels. Shem and I did our best to keep up, slipping and sliding through the snow with the icy cold turning our hands into icicles. So began the great battle for Creature Kingdom. It was a wildfire of a ride, so hold on tight.

CHAPTER EIGHT

You hanging on? Because it was then that all of hell and Hades broke loose. We got out of Creaky Forest, but not without a band of evil sounding horns blasting into the night, signaling the compromise of forest security. In no time, a band of rats riding on bobcats sped out of the Creaky Forest in pursuit of our rear ends, carrying flaming torches and aiming bows and arrows after us. They were especially trained for prison break-outs, based on their speed and malice. One might even call them the Creaky Coup. The rats had eyes like red fire and unnaturally long tails which some of them brandished as whips and swung to and fro above their heads like they was some kind of demonic cowboys. It was tough running in the snow. I slipped and fell more than a few times, and wouldn't have made it far if Shem hadn't helped me to my feet time and again. The critters, since they had no weapons to fight with, kept on running straight North towards a thick copse of pure white birch trees, frigid and silver in the star-light. We had about three hundred yards to cross by the looks of it.

"We get in there and we'll be safe for the time being!" cried the Colonel. "To the Birches!"

"The Birches!!" we all bellowed, with the demon rats closing in fast. By and by, a familiar sounding shot shook the atmosphere, and a flaming snowball exploded just a few feet ahead of us, throwing up a blinding wall of snow and smoke. The Colonel reeled to a stop and turned around. There was pure rage and death in his eyes, a sight I don't care to recall, to tell the honest truth. "They've got my blunderbuss," he said. I didn't know the particular story behind the Colonel and his cherished weapon, but by the way he talked of it, seemed like the two of them nearly had an emotional bond, like a daddy and his child.

"Colonel!" I called after him. "Get it later! Now ain't the time! Let it go, c'mon, quick, or ye'll git yerself cudgeled by that thing!" But there warn't no convincing him. Quick as a lightning bolt, the Colonel zipped off, head on against the dozen or so rat riders. He dodged arrows and stones. A projectile hit an antler, and still he kept on like a charging elk. He had his eyes trained on the foremost rider, a massive rat with blood red eyes and a tongue that wagged out the side of its mouth, limp and purple in the wind. "It's Fiddleback," the Colonel said to himself, and leaped about twenty feet in the air with the antlers poised at an angle for the kill. I ain't never seen the likes of it in my whole measly sojourn on the earth.

Fiddleback snarled at the offender, and both he and the bobcat he was riding slid to a stop and gaped at the meteoric jackalope sailing right towards them. Fiddleback lifted the blunderbuss, snickering with delight as the target honed in, but didn't live to pull the trigger, for the shot of a pistol rang out in the dark from the steady hand of Shem Tellingsworth, who was standing poised and sublime a whole thirty yards away at the edge of the Birches. If that boy don't beat all.

The rat fell dead into the snow and the rest of the riders ducked and cussed us out, then sped back to Creaky Forest like a shadow on the snow. We were kneeling and panting at the foot of the birch forest with branches that looked like silver fuses reaching out, electrified, into the night sky. The bare branches were all coated with ice, so they glistened and rustled in the moonlight and evening wind.

"Everyone all right?" asked the Colonel, arriving on the scene while cleaning the blunderbuss with his paw. He glanced at Shem, nodded his thanks, and turned back to the critters. We all nodded, said yeah, we were fine, but doggone tired.

"We've come to the right place," said the Colonel, softly. "They won't follow us in here."

The company slowly walked into the trees, finding that somehow it was lighter and warmer inside its boundaries, though the air still stung our faces with coldness. A dark stream trickled through the snow. There were no owls or crows in the trees, nor squirrel nests or leaves. The bark was pale and bare, the snow gathered in sloping hills against the slender trunks. The silence of the place seemed imbued in the trees themselves, like it was the language they spoke to one another, and expected any passersby to abide by the quiet as well. And we did. The whole crew walked as if upon a sacred pearl of great price, like it was a planet no one had ever set foot on, and maybe never would again. I don't believe I have ever felt so reverent nor so at peace in my whole life. Shem was in wonder at it all, too. His eyes were glass in the moonlight, mouth open wide. I smiled, tiredly. I had misread the boy, no doubt. Old Tate was right about that young buck. World ain't gone totally to pot, yet.

We continued farther until we reached somewhat of a clearing and decided this was as good as any to make up a fire and try to get some sleep. Fortunately, some of the freed-critters had brought along their bedding from their old cells, and raided the storage for pillows and quilts whilst the Colonel had given his speech. Some critters are just attendant as busybees to basic necessities like that, and Lord love them for it. Afore long we'd all spread out our blankets and huddled around a blazing fire, feeling safe and secure and even warm in the center of the Silver Birches. I don't believe I've ever slept better in all my days.

The next morning, a clear, golden light fell through the Silver Birches and alighted on us where we lay. I opened my eyes, lashes rimmed with frost, and sat up to look around. The air smelled clear, fresh, and woody, and the stream gurgled a few feet behind me. I heard the clear whistle of an osprey a mile above me and the gentlest wind rinse the forest just a foot above me. Through the veil of birches, I could make out the surrounding field and the many hills behind it, gray and wooded and mysterious. The Creature

Kingdom. The Colonel was awake next and took the opportunity to polish his gun again and then tramp off to drink some water from the stream. By and by the rest of the crew was leaning up on their elbows, rubbing their eyes. Most of them looked genuinely confused to have woken up in a place like the Silver Fuse, when all they'd been used to was those dank cells in Creaky Forest. It must've been a right regenerative surprise, I wagered. Some of them was evening pinching themselves for happiness. "Free at last," a little lady squirrel murmured to herself. "I wonder if my boy Bill is still in Post Oak Office . . . and Sid still carting trout down the river." Not only had young Shem freed my own hide from the throes of darkness, but he'd restored these here creatures to their old lives of normal living, and that ain't no small achievement.

"Well, what's our next move, chief?" I asked the Colonel.

"I expect we need reinforcements," he said. "We need troops, artillery, archers and chariot riders. The whole she-bang."

"I'll be darned."

"These kidnappings ought to be an act of war against both our kinfolk, Arnie Tuck. Ain't no two ways about it. We're in outright civil war."

"Well, in that case, we ought to go to Jimmytown, at least Shem and I, to gather some proper weaponry and steeds."

"I don't reckon there'll be time, sadly."

"How do ye reckon?"

"Your friends, that were snatched by the Duke. They was trespassin' on what that vampire bobcat considers his sacred territory, by conquest. I fear that they're in mortal danger, Arnie, if we don't seek to set them free at once."

"Can't we get more critters?" I asked. "And what about Bigfoot? I must say, I figured on seein' him come around by now."

"The king'll show up in his own good time, as he always does," said the Colonel, brows knitted. "But if we always rely on him to save the day for us, well, we wouldn't never act on our own." The Colonel turned to Shem and said, "You certain ye heard right, son, about the Duke takin' the men to the Ghoul's Gambit?"

Shem nodded. "Yes sir, that's right. Sure as can be." The Colonel sighed. "That's the Ghoul's wretched domain—it's an old, abandoned house at its center, with lots of bastions build around it. Every year, more trees fall, more trenches are dug, more labor from kidnapped critters needed to build the Gambit." He paused to think. "There's an old armory in Camaroo's Curtain, and it's a halfway point between the Gambit and Creature Kingdom. If we can get supplied there, we can carry on to the Gambit. But we need troops!" The Colonel stood up, watching the creatures and gnomes as they began to roll up their packs and blow their warm breath into their paws. Suddenly, at the edge of the silver birches and behind the company, the figure of a gray fox appeared, a paw poised in front of his chest and green eyes set right on us. It was heaving for breath, and its fur was all puffed out in every direction. The Colonel saw him same time I did and jumped for joy. "Of course! The detective—he lives in the Silver Birches. My dear friend!" The Colonel and "detective" galloped towards each other until they gave each other full on hugs and noogies, like they hadn't seen each other for ages. "Dear old Sidney!" said the fox in a thick southern Savannah accent. "What is the meanin' of this company of critters? And the two humans?"

"Oh, there's lots to tell, Jethro, but the Creaky Forest prison, so long under the key of the Gray Vulture, has been broken into, and the prisoners released!" He proceeded to catch Jethro up on the all the goings on, including how he'd met me on the "other side" of Hogback Creek, and how we'd been taken into custody, only to have this brave young feller of a human break us out and lead us to the haven of the silver birches.

"I'll be! These poor souls look like they need a proper fire and breakfast."

"That they do. I'm glad to see you, Jethro. This here is Arnie Tuck, and Shem Tellingsworth, residents of the fair city of Jimmytown." It was certainly the first time I ever shook paws with a fox, and if you can believe it, wouldn't be last neither! "Pleased to make your acquaintance, gentlemen," said Jethro, bowing his head. He was wearing, I noticed, a silver monocle over his eye, and a small green vest that hung unbuttoned over his neck with a wooden pipe dangling out of the chest pocket. Looked like this particular fox was something of a cultured critter, a "renaissance fox," may we say.

"You've probably heard by now about the sad incident regardin' the Jimmytown fellers over at Bobblehead Wood?" said the Colonel.

"Indeed I have. And by the hand of a human." Jethro's deep, sonorous voice got all the more solemn as he went on. "The penalty for trespassing, in the Ghoul's eyes, that is, a serious offense. Don't ask me why. It's like, if the humans were to get pulled over for speedin', puttin' them in jail for the rest of their lives."

"We need to bring the fight to them," said the Colonel. The detective rubbed his chin, glanced at the company of animals once more, then raised a thoughtful claw and said, "Here's what I propose, gents. I lead these tired critters back to Creature Kingdom and get some food in their bellies, and then go straight to the Kingdom Commons to alert the Secretary of Defense of the situation. Sam's his name. He's a good old goat, and he'll know what do to. We'll assemble to cavalry and infantry and march on the Gambit together. Ain't just the humans in there, mind ye, but countless of our own citizens, trapped and enslaved by the Ghoul. Some've been there for years, and we've plumb failed them up until now. It's time to join forces and march together."

"Can ye get there by tonight?" said the Colonel. "We can't waste one lick of time."

"If I don't make it, ye can set my tail afire," said Jethro. He turned to the company and called on them all to follow him back to Creature Kingdom.

The freed-critters looked at each other hesitantly, until finally the little red fox who we first freed perked up and said, "Excuse me, Detective, but I think I speak on behalf of all my fellow, friendly beasts that we want to join ranks in the fight—seein' that we were freed from prison, we think it only right to try and help all those other poor lads out too." He paused as his comrades all nodded along in agreement. "And, well, I dunno about everyone else here, but I'd be right ashamed to go on home at a time like this. If the situation is so dire as the good Colonel says, well, looks like it's off to battle!" Jethro, understandably a bit surprised, listened to the crew bark and mew and hoot their cheers. "Time's a wastin'!" they cried out. "We got to save Arnie and Shem's folks!!"

"They've got a point, Ro," murmured the Colonel.

It was at that moment that an unexpected feller approached our ranks. He slid out from one of the trees quiet as could be, and looked skeert to the bone, poor bugger. It was a small black bear, and he was carrying a note in his paw, raising it and trying to gather our attention. Jethro noticed him after a few seconds and trotted over to see what the matter was. He knew the bear. Remmy was his name. He was a good old bear, apparently, if sometimes absent-minded in his wanderings. Everyone quieted down while Jethro listened to Remmy whisper something in his ear. He passed the note into the fox's paw and then lumbered away through the birches 'til his backside vanished beyond a snowdrift. I reckon these talking bears skip the whole hibernating session and keep on rolling through life with their kin, which I find right admirable. Anyways, the Detective unfolded the paper, adjusted his monocle, and began to read for the listening audience: "To those concerned, it has come to my attention that the woeful prisoners of the Creaky Forest have escaped! If the human, that dastardly Arnie Tuck, wants to see his dear friends again, you will march those prisoners to the Ghoul Gambit and hand them over, and we'll be happy to oblige an exchange. If you fail to do so by the end of this *very* evening, let me be clear: those men won't see tomorrow's dawn. Signed: the immanent *Duke Deuchamp Domchomp the 17th* (or *Dew Dommy Doo Doo* for short)." Jethro crumpled the paper in his paw. We were all silent and still, not knowing what to say. Of all the wicked ways of breathing organisms under the sun, this topped the utmost notch. There was a fire inside Shem's eye, and his jawbone was working something fierce. He glanced at me, eyes swimming with tears, and whispered, "Sir, my daddy's among them. 'Mong the captured." I gripped his shoulder as the tears fell. "I should've

tried to save *him* when I had the chance. And with mama havin'
the baby soon . . . "

"Hush now, son. Don't you worry," I said. "We'll get him out
of there. Don't you worry."

"Well, this changes things," said the Detective.

"I don't see why," said the Colonel, defiantly as ever. "I say we
go straight to the Gambit. If we start now, we'll make it by evening,
and I'll shoot my blunderbuss bullets high into the sky so all of
Creature Kingdom knows there's a fight for lives and souls to be
had. I say it again . . . bring the fight to them!!" A raucous cheer
arose from every critter's mouth, while a radiant grin spread over
the Detective's face and all the silver birches seemed to clap and
cheer along with them like there was something holy synergy betwixt critter, root, snow, and wind.

So, it was decided. We would head to the armory and then
into the Ghoul's Gambit, where I must confide, I was a bit afeard to
come near. I was leaving Jimmytown behind. I was walking away
from Mindy, my true love, and my darling kiddos. But I thought
of Shem's pappy. Of Old Man Scooter and Barber Charlie. And I
thought of Old Tate, laying close to death back home, in need of
his friends by his side during the last moments. The fathers and
brothers and sons of Jimmytown were at stake. I gritted my teeth
and clapped Shem on the shoulder.

"C'mon, son. It's a new day, full of glory and the good Lord's
joy. And we live in a right ornery universe at that."

CHAPTER NINE

T HE company of soldiers, I guess it now was, set out from the Silver Birches. We were instantly faced with a harsh wind sweeping down from the east, though the day was clear and the sun was already well risen above the hills. It was still well below freezing, with the wind being probably into the negatives. I tightened my old corduroy coat around myself, lined with sheep's wool, tighter round myself and wondered how far it was to the armory. Turned out it warn't far at all. The Colonel led us up into the hill country again, where the trees are of sycamore and birch and cedar and even some pine, but I couldn't see no birds nor hear no streams running there. We went on quietly and with a keen eye afore us. The Colonel always had a "finger" resting on the trigger of his blunderbuss, and Lord know he was ready for any assault which might come our way. Shem had his pistol in a holster at his belt, looking a bit tired and somewhat afeard.

"Ye all right, son?" I whispered.

He started at the voice, then smiled. "Oh. Yessir I'm all right. Just . . . well, ye know. I didn't exactly expect to be assaulting ghouls with a load of worn-out beasts of the forest."

"Amen to that, son," I said, chuckling. "This beats all, no two ways about it. But ye know, won't it be a time goin' on home after all this comes to a head and tell the story around the fire?"

Shem smiled. "Yessir. That will be a good old time." He was quiet, biting his lip and running a hand through his hair. "This ghoul I hear tell of," he said. "Well, it simply sounds devilish, sir, and I must admit I ain't so keen on seein' this Gambit, or whatever they callin' in. If this critter is as evil as they say, will we even get to *go* home?"

"I hear ye, son," I said. And I did hear him, loud and clear. Ain't no one in the cosmos that's naturally inclined to face off with wicked forces, but sometimes, ye ain't got much of a choice, and we have to do the best we can to fight it when it rears its ugly brow against the ones we love. I was on the verge of telling Shem as much, and going off with some platitude of wisdom, parellelling the likes of Plato and Arsetotle and Some-crates, but for some reason or another it didn't seem like the proper anecdote. So I goes, "Shem, there's much in this strange world which is beyond our reckonin.' And sometimes folks do things for which there ain't no explanation. Like Japheth. I knew the boy when he was just a youngster, and I 'member all he e'er wanted was fer his daddy to be proud of him. His daddy was a strong feller in town—proud, loud, defiant. He got in fights at the saloon and would go home purty well beat up. And what did he say to young Japheth? Can't no one know fer sure, but it probably warn't no praise and adoration. And take that there bobcat duke vampire, Dew Dommy Doo Doo. Ye maybe saw him cart off our brethren into the night. Well, the Colonel was childhood buddies with the critter, sure as shoelace. They was brothers, nearly. What happened? There ain't no tellin' for sure, son, but we know this—whether the Nameless Ghoul or the prince of the power of the air or what have ye, there's always forces beyond mere human decision which play a part in the grand story of ordinary life and chance. And we got a choice to make. Which side we'll fight for and against."

"What's the other side? The other way?" Shem asked. "Seems like this ghoul is all powerful. In a way. Seems that just about everybody falls into his clutches in one way or another. In the end, I mean."

"Well, I'd grant ye that if I was convinced that there warn't nothin' else deeper, brighter, and truer than the gloom and darkness of this world," I said. "Sometimes it seems like ye said—that there ain't no resistin' the wicked bents ye see all around, and in yourself. Lord knows that there ain't no one who don't have the potential to be a Japheth or a Dew Dommy or a ghoul. But at some point ye'll have to decide just what's lyin' at the very heart of the equation. What's at the center of the universe? What tree roots go down deeper than a water hungry cedar or one of them Californey redwoods?"

"I don't know," Shem said, though he sounded a little more hopeful.

"'Tis the power of love, sonny," I said. "The kind of love which compelled ye to charge through the Creaky Forest and save an old fool like me. The love for which I've got burnin' in me for Sammie, Bobby, and Mindy. The kind of power that don't want to take nothin' from nobody, but give and give for the fillin' up of others, even if it means dyin' and lettin' go. That's the kind of power that Old Tate and I discovered when we looked into the eyes of Bigfoot. The creature warn't a monster, but a lover—a beast in love with the woods, the snow, the stars, the kingdom of all things lovely and right and good and holy. And that's the power we got on our side now."

Shem didn't say nothing, but seemed to let loose a shiver of relief, and smiled. By then we were well up the hill and could see the armory fold into view. It was made up of white stones stacked upon one another, with a thatched roof and a heavy wooden door under an archway at its center. It was surrounded by thick post oaks and birch trees, pale and straight and strong, like quiet guardians. The Colonel cleared the drift of snow away from the base of the door, revealing the words engraved in capital letters through the center: CAMAROO'S CURTAIN.

"We're here," said Jethro. The fox tinkered with some keys from his front pocket and took out a long silver one. He stuck it gingerly into the keyhole on the door and, with the help of a couple of stags, urged it forward. We all filed slowly inside, smelling mothballs and mustiness within. There was a window in the center of each wall, letting in the silver light and revealing columns of all sorts of weaponry, much of which I'd imagine belonged with King Arthur of the Dark Ages. There was little catapults and sling-shots and spears and cannonballs, along with bows and arrows and curved scimitars. Some of it was a mite rusted over, but still in strong condition, all things considered. "Okay, critters, arm up—accordin' to size and capacity, mind ye," said the Colonel. "And look here! They still got their winter reserves from the Ten-Year Feud. Ah . . . dried cranberry and Nutmeg oats with coriander seed. Oooh—my favorite! Some salted almonds." So, we all had at the stores of food, which was a real blessing seeing we was all feeling right starved. By the looks of it, most of the prisoners had forgotten how to properly eat their food. Like they didn't know what to do with so much food for the taking. We all could eat our fill and get all the way to four and five servings each, fueled for battle in both body and soul.

"Very well, gentle-creatures," said the Detective, shouldering what they call a Filligan's Flute, which can shoot Filligan stones faster than a cobra can bite, and leaning against the door. "Listen up, y'all. The Colonel and I, bein' the most, shall we say, knowl-edgeable of the gee-hography around these parts, will be leadin' this valiant brigade. Camaroo's Curtain is the last free forest west of the Gambit, so breathe it all in whilst ye can." I must say the southern accent come off the fox's lips sweet and deep and slow like sonorous jazz mixed with honey, and it was a sonic pleasure to listen to him no matter *what* he said. "When we come across the hill, you're gonna see the cursed camp. Now the Ghou's 'castle,' as he calls it, is right smack dab in the center of the place, fortified by bobcat sentries, and w'arwolves too. This ain't no picnic, now. Sur-roundin' the place are barracks and buildings studded with fenc-ing. They're cuttin' trees down by the forest-full, and the Curtain is their next target. Now ye don't need me to tell ye that this ain't just an assault. It's a *rescue* mission. The Duke kidnapped the crew of humans and aims to use them as leverage ag'in us. Well, cute of him. He can pat himself on the back and twit around as the

Ghoul's lackey if he wants to, but see here—ain't nobody goin' to meddle as such with folks no longer." Jethro squinted his green eyes and slightly grinned. "Bigfoot has promised us aid when we're in a pinch, ain't he?"

"But sir," said a small brown bunny who kept wringing her paws. "Nobody's seen him for so long. How do we know he still loves us? That he still cares?"

Jethro glanced at me, the grin widening a bit, and he winked. "Because the King promised us he does, dear madam," he said, softly. "And he appears exactly when he means to, and to exactly *whom* he means to."

CHAPTER TEN

HERE we come to the p'int of the tale in which you may want to turn back. I'd understand, right honestly, I would. The things which I'm about to relate really happened, and something like them may rightly happen again. There ain't no telling. But I must say that the worst woes have the potential for the best victories, so mayhaps it's worth sticking 'round.

We continued through Camaroo's Curtain in a single file line with the Colonel and Detective and the helm and Shem and I close on their heels. Everyone was armed and nourished, and the 'drenaline was pumping intensely in every critter's veins and hearts. The woods were strangely quiet, like they were a pair of giant lungs unwilling to exhale—it was too suspenseful to do anything but wait and stay quiet. We had no specific plan. Once over the hill, the bowmen would launch their missiles and the foot soldiers would off and flank the camp and do paw to paw combat when the time came, whilst Shem and I were to make our way straight for the "pit" where undoubtedly all the boys were being held against their will. Our chances of success? Nary a percentage. Our will to succeed? Overflowing like Niagara Falls, except with the potency of a million rivers more! We come up to the top of the hill and the Colonel held up a paw, elbow crooked, signaling us to stop. We did so, and if it was quiet afore then, it became the silence of a grave now.

"All right soldiers," the Detective whispered. "On my count." He raised his hind leg, and upon the third time it touched the ground, we'd charge the hill. One, two . . . Jethro's green eyes smiled and shone in the midday sun . . . THREE! With a passionate war whoop, the Creature Kingdom brigade swarmed over the hill, each to his proper station. The archers lined up in a row and immediately started to let them have it, whilst the rest of us flew downward in the snow towards the dastardly settlement. And a gloomy sight it was, too, lemme tell ye. The "castle" was indeed in the center of the establishment. It was a tall, rickety edifice, several stories high, with a broad front porch and covered in dead ivy. The house looked like it was once painted a sort of cream color, but now it was simply scratched up and charred with smoke stains and yeller marks. That was the funny thing, see. This might've once been a peaceable farmhouse at one point in time. Heck, perhaps it belonged to one of my personal ancestors, seeing my kin did actually move over to Jimmytown from across the creek back in the day. But look at what it had turned into. All the trees had been bull dozed to the ground within a hundred yards diameter and made into cabin-like barracks all around so it looked like a city establishment on the rise. And who would've thunk? They'd used all the tractors from Jimmytown and Shady Ridge to do the destruction, and there was bobcats driving pickup trucks roundabout the way with rifles slung over their shoulders and wearing coonskin caps. If that don't beat all. Plus, there was the w'arwolves. Now a w'arwolf is one of them devilish beasts that I simply detest to the core. They're gangly and too humanoid for comfort but have all the markings of a monster, hunched and mangy, drooling all over the place and pacing the ground about. Of course, there warn't any there at present because of the lack of a full moon, but if I looked close I could see their beady eyes peeping from underneath the barracks, waiting. But to be honest, the strangest sight I laid eyes on whilst charging the barricades wasn't no monster nor foul critter. It wasn't even the Ghoul itself. It was a man, tied up to a post just outside the Gambit's porch, blindfolded and with a paper crown jammed down on his head. "Good Lord," I whispered. "It's Japheth."

And it was, too. As the arrows flew and the Gambit scattered and fled to reorganize and fight back, I could see Japheth struggling against his bonds, teeth gritted and brow knitted. He wore nothing except his long underwear, which made him look all the more goofy, and also his boots. With these he stamped the ground, trying to get loose. Scrawled on an unkempt board above his head was the sentence: "Mayor of Jimmytown!" That poor son of a gun. He'd been duped into betraying his own just to get humiliated as a prize. I didn't know at that time that he'd been promised the mayor's seat, but it was purty clear what had happened. The Ghoul hated humans—all of them, even the back stabbers. He just wanted to make sport of them. And for some reason that made me all the more furious.

We got the edge on the Gambit. The archers done a good job of pinpointing their targets, and the catapults we'd hauled along were starting to do some damage on the barracks, even on the house itself. But the element of surprise is a short-lived companion, and military strategy only benefits from it for a limited spell. It warn't long afore the enemy had their own catapults steadied and aimed, and let fly a torrent of flaming snowballs towards the archers. The Colonel called on them to stand their ground but find cover where they may and fired his blunderbuss with his trademark precision into the Gambit's heart. The foot soldiers, meanwhile, had flanked the encampment successfully and were ready to scramble up the remaining ditch and over the makeshift barbwire fence. But by then we too were attracting fire and had to duck as we crept along. Shem popped a couple of shots with his pistol, taking out a weasel or two. The aim of this kid ain't failed to impress me yet!

The real trouble was staying protected from obliteration once *inside* the Gambit itself. The prisoner's pit was right behind the castle and would surely be swarming with guards. We needed our archers and sharpshooters to do some keen sniping, that was certain. We clumb up the ditch, the artillery whizzing above our heads, and Jethro let his tail bristle. There was about fifty critters with us total. Every one of us was prepared to give up our lives for the greater good. For there was more than humans being kept and enslaved beyond the fence. This was everybody's fight.

"I can't promise all will go well up there," said Jethro. How that voice of his carried so! "But I can promise ye that I'll put my neck out fer any creature in mortal danger. If yer trapped, holler, and someone will come. Every critter for every other critter. Swell?" We all nodded. The Colonel had caught up with us while the archers continued to rain terror abundant, and patted my shoulder with a gentle paw. "I'm glad to have met ye, Arnie Tuck," he whispered in my ear. "And I'm proud to fight alongside ye, even if 'tis our final hullabaloo."

"The honor's all mine, Colonel," I replied.

He smiled at me. "Remember me by my name, if you can: Sidney Roscoe's the ring." With that, he and Jethro leaped over the edge of the ditch and beyond the fence in an acrobatic swirl of brown and gray, antler and tail, landing cleanly on enemy soil. One of our catapults obliterated a piece of the fence shortly thereafter, paving a way for the brigade to pour into the Gambit unimpeded. "To the pit!" I bellowed, with Shem close by me, shooting weasels and demon rats by the dozens.

I must confess that a battle of such chaos is hard to fully account for. It's like time itself gets suspended. Every second is an eternity, each movement full of consequence. I guess you could say all of life gets sped up and heightened in a battle, and that the realities of the world compress and become vividly real, all in the intensity, the motion, the noise. And those are the realities of life and death, and the fragile thread running betwixt them. Death can no longer be ignored, or denied, but becomes what it's always been to the mortal human beings: the main course of the meal. But you know, it was like I was telling young Shem earlier that very day. There *are* some things which are stronger and deeper and brighter than death and gloom. If there warn't, well—what we were doing fighting against it? And that was the thought which drove us on against the gathering ranks of rebels, giving us strength and stamina even as our own critters started to fall.

The archers streamed in after us, pulling out their scimitars and crossbows for short range. We had caught the Gambit by such surprise that we were able to push them past their outer barracks and closer towards the Ghoul's tower. I could still see Japheth at the post, although he looked to have fainted, or froze. One or the other. We were making gains. The enemy was plumb scared and scrambling as we pressed on, 'til the brigade was right up against the front porch, so they had to nearly go inside for their safety. See, it turned out that many of the troops were out domineering other parts of free nature, and warn't present to help their foul Master at home camp. Dew Dommy Doo Doo was there, though, biting and scratching something awful, and hissing every which way with fury. "You will pay for your treachery!" he kept wheezing. "You'll see! You'll regret it!!"

All was looking on our side. Could it have been so easy? I do sincerely wish it were. Just as we were getting ready to start breaking into the Ghoul's abode, we felt a shudder of atmosphere ripple through us, like an earthquake of the soul. The air seemed to darken, and a coldness that wasn't quite physical shrouded the air above us. We hesitated, and everyone stopped their fighting. Japheth was softly whimpering. "I'm sorry, Arnie," he whispered. I glanced at him. "I didn't know what I was in for . . . honestly I didn't . . . the Ghoul . . . promised me everything. Power. Women. The mayor-ship . . . " His face contorted in pain. "Ye know. Things that my daddy would have seen and said, 'Wow, that's mighty fine, son. Ye done made somethin' of yourself." I nodded.

"The other men, where they at?" I asked.

Wind started to blow bitterly through the camp. "Behind the house," he said. "Arnie . . . I'm sorry."

The eeriness met its climax when the source of the shadow showed up in the Gambit's very doorway. The Ghoul, or Nameless, as I guess we should call him, was not quite what I expected. He was hooded in a nearly transparent, gray robe, showing flashes of a skeletal underbelly, and held a reaper's scythe in one hand. His eyes were white fire, thin and cruel, and one could only spot his mouth when he spoke. The words come out of a black hole, and seemed to suck air in as they released. I got the notion that Nameless wasn't all the way *real* or *present,* which made the presence that he did have all the more ominous, if you read me. Here was a critter who once was, but had chosen to exist as less than real, if only he could wield power over the living.

A nearby bunny shot an arrow at the Ghoul, but it wisped right through him and sunk itself into the wooden doorway right behind his head. Nameless hissed out some wretched laugh, and raised the scythe in one hand as if preparing to strike.

"You fools," he said in a whisper. "Come to rescue your friends? Your friends are beyond your reach." He drifted forward, forcing us to all back up a few yards into the snow. I found myself next to Japheth again. He was gasping for breath, eyes shut tight. "Don't look at him too long," he whispered to me. "Don't look at him too long. Ye won't be able to see anything right if ye do." From then on I did my best to stare at the ground in front of me as the Ghoul swept back and forth in front of our trembly ranks. "Creatures fall and die. Buildings burn and crash. But Ghouls? Ghouls never die."

Duke Domchamp had slunk behind his master's ethereal cloak, head bowed. "My Lord," he mewed. "Shall we deposit them in the pit with the others?"

"In a moment." The Ghoul approached the post, staring into Japheth's closed eyes, and ran a bony finger down the boy's stubbly chin. Japheth went notably pale at the touch. "First, an exhibition of the traitor's demise. We'll bring them out one by one . . . "

"You'll won't do nothin' of the sort, Ghoul."

The words were spoken clear and musical-like just a few feet behind us. We all spun on our heels, forgetting even the Ghoul, and I'll be barbecued: it was the glorious Bigfoot, standing ten feet tall and wearing a green and gold cape. His eyes were golden, blue, and green, and the smell of forest and river and snow came off like mountain wind from his fur. He carried no weapon but was holding a wood staff in his hand-paw. Even whilst standing in the midst of perilous foes, seeing the majestic critter done set me back on Scraggly Hill with Old Tate where we'd first laid eyes on him. I was transported, and nothing else really seemed to matter.

The Ghoul gave a hideous shriek, but, thinking quick, drew the scythe right up next to Japheth's throat and hissed, "Not a step closer, you hateful animal. The blood of traitors and slaves rightfully belongs to me—don't you remember? This man deserves to die. In my humble opinion, *all* these cursed humans and critters of the fold deserve it, but they'll all have their proper time."

Japheth managed to open his eyes just a smidgen, so that he saw Bigfoot standing there right in front of him. The "monster" he'd aimed to turn into a rug became a figure of power and destiny. His lip trembled. He must've known that he didn't have much a case aimed in his favor. He was a thief, a womanizer, and a loveless traitor to boot. I'll admit I personally warn't feeling so lovey-dovey towards him myself at the moment.

"If ye kill the boy, the crimes are done away, and you can release the rest of the men and Creature Kingdom citizens you've stolen," said Bigfoot. "That's true, all right."

"Ahh, now you're talking legality."

"But tell me, this Ghoul." We all turned an ear to listen to what was coming next. Every eye was fixed on the king. "Which would you rather have? The traitor, a boy who stumbled into your grasp unwittingly . . . or me?" At that, the whole crowd gasped.

"No, King!" cried the Colonel. "You can't be serious! By my life, you'll never do such a thing!"

"Quiet, dear old jackalope," replied Bigfoot. He turned back to the Ghoul, who had lowered the blade and was staring intently at the sasquatch with an ever-growing gleam of evil in his eye. "The only catch is this," Bigfoot continued. "You not only release Japheth, but *all* those you've kidnapped and enslaved." Nameless twitched and hissed, but said, "Be it one freed or seven hundred, it doesn't matter if the King himself is dead! Duke, cut the man down." Dew Dommy did as he was told. Japheth fell to his knees in the snow, rubbing his wrists and quietly weeping. Personally, I was dumbstruck to the core. How could I not be? Bigfoot was giving himself up to the dark powers? Not a mite of it made sense.

It simply made no faluting sense to my line of reasoning and sensibilities. Japheth was the one who had hated, stolen, lied, and lusted. He was the one who'd brought pain on our community, put discord amongst the Bigfoot Brethren.

"Tie up the beast, soldiers." The Ghoul scrutinized the king's every move as a band of bobcats and stump gnomes waddled on over to take off Bigfoot's cape and lead him to the post. Bigfoot didn't resist. He didn't even make one suspicious move, although he looked strong enough to turn the whole place upside down with just one punch of the fist. As he was being tied with Japheth's bonds, he looked down on me, and a light of recognition passed over his face. I was searching for the words to say but came up empty.

"Arnie, ain't it?" Bigfoot said.

"That's right, sir. I'm the hillbilly who spotted you just the other week, near Hogback Creek."

"And now you're fighting to free my critters." His smile grew wider. "You're an honorable feller."

"But Bigfoot, sir, I don't understand. Why are you givin' yourself up for such a feller as Japheth?"

Bigfoot was quiet as the final knot was tied. The Jimmytown men appeared from behind the house, rubbing their sore arms and blinking at the light of the sun. "Don't despise him, Arnie," said Bigfoot. "If you can, go so far as to forgive him!" Japheth had risen to his feet and stared in wonder at the Bigfoot he'd wanted so long to kill. Now the glorious beast was bound secure on the traitor's post, and if he had the chance, he very well could've been the one to do the killing. "Thank you," he said, softly. "I don't deserve to live on."

"That's the only way *to* live, sonny," said Bigfoot. "By seein' that you don't deserve it."

"Away, wretched fiends!" screamed the Ghoul. "Go before I change my mind and slay you all!"

The Colonel and Detective wouldn't budge, but Bigfoot nodded towards them and said, "Do as he says, old friends. It's the only way."

"I would have stood by you to the very end," wept the Colonel. "And you have. Go!"

Slowly, we went from that place in a bittersweet exodus. The prisoners embraced the critters they hadn't seen for so long. Family members reunited, tears of joy and thanksgiving were shed. I was relieved for the safety of the boys, though they were tuckered out and more'n ready to go home. Shem and his daddy, Samuel, walked together, speaking in low voices, Samuel's arm around his son's shoulder. "I'm so proud of you, son," I heard him say. "Thank you."

Japheth, meanwhile, dawdled a ways behind us, and no one was speaking to him yet. But I couldn't stand it. We were at the top of the hill going into Camaroo's Curtain, and I looked back on the Ghoul's Gambit, a smoking, desolate place, wounded by the attack but still crawling with that malicious power. I saw the Ghoul raise that cursed blade of his, pause for a moment as if musing on his fortune, and bring it down with a vengeance across Bigfoot's open chest. Light flashed, and clouds formed above, and the snow swept into the valley so I couldn't see nothing more.

CHAPTER ELEVEN

I T behooves us to end this tale on a note of hymnody. And even though what you just read may be a mixed bag of berries, I promise this parting word is a feast through and through. Two weeks later, it was Christmas Eve, and Jimmytown was alight in all its holiday glory. Multicolored lights were strung up between the buildings, carolers sung to no end on the walks, and we had our Glory Tree up and tall in the town square.

Now it's the hillbilly tradition around these parts to invite every living creature within ten miles to the Christmas Banquet, and since I'd made some new friends recently, that meant some new seats was needed. Mindy wasn't all excited to hear that I'd invited a number of squirrels and b'ars to the banquet, but she was so grateful to God that I'd survived the Ghoul's Gambit that she conceded. And now that all the fellers in town had seen the sights alongside me, pretty soon everyone was convinced: Bigfoot was a real stand-up critter, and the other side of the creek was worth befriending.

Mr. Ham, since the school was out for Christmas holiday, was spending a whole lot of time in his personal quarters above the movie-house, and though I wouldn't have minded for him to stay there amongst his volumes and tomes, Mindy demanded I invite him to Christmas.

"It ain't right, that boy bein' all alone for the holidays," she said. E'er since I come back from the other side of the creek, a rugged war hero, mind ye, she refused to be more than a few inches away from my side. She clung to me even then, and then here come Bobby and Sammie too, engulfing me in an ocean of familial affection. "All right, then," I said. "If ye say so."

The night Shem and I got back into Jimmytown and the Colonel and Detective led the critters back to the Creature Kingdom, Shem, after stumbling in search of the words, told me, "Seein' how—well, I dunno—I ain't got much use for the spotlight, sir, would ye mind keepin' mum about my involvement in all this? Would ye not tell Sammie of it, sir?" I was surprised, since I'd been planning on preaching Shem's valor to the whole town and beyond, but when I saw the sincerity in the request, I said, "Sure thing, Shem. But I reckon someday ye ought to tell her of what ye did. 'Member, bein' humble don't mean lyin' about yourself. It just means refusin' to tote your taters for more than they're worth."

Shem paused, then nodded. "Yes sir."

"Mighty proud of you, son," said Samuel.

"That makes the two of us," I added.

I visited Mr. Ham in his room on Christmas Eve, right afore the banquet, and found him bent over a book thick as a pig. He looked tired, and was unkempt in his attire, which was a stark contrast from how he portrayed himself out in the open. There was an empty bottle of wine at his feet and some magazines scattered on the rug. The room itself was a mess, and you couldn't even see the desk beneath all the papers, books, ink splotches, and coffee stains.

"Oh," he said, straightening up and setting the book by his feet. "Mr. Tuck. Please come in. What a pleasant surprise."

I took off my hat and thanked him, then looked him square in the eye as he stood up to try and match my stature. "You're invited to the Christmas Banquet in the chapel hall," I said. "You sincerely should join us."

He nodded. "Thank you for the invitation, though I don't usually do well in social gatherings. Who will all be in attendance?"

"Oh, just about everybody in town," I replied. I didn't mention the many critters who'd made it on our VIP list, thinking this might seriously dissuade the feller.

"Ah."

"But you'll sit with me and Mindy, so you'll have some familiarity to jive with." He was quiet, and I turned to go. "You should come," I said. "Come eat with Jimmytown."

"I'll think about it. Thank you."

In the street below, I looked up to see Mr. Ham standing in the window, a solitary silhouette lifting the curtain so he could get a view of the street and the folks who were starting to populate it. He dropped it as soon as he saw me peering up at him, and I walked on over to the chapel hall.

It was a mighty fine party, let me tell you. Every person in town brought something, whether pies or beets or tomato whiskey or honey ham or mistletoe to pin in the archways. The whole town was there, along with a fair amount of folks from Shady Ridge over the hills. And, not to mention the critters. Jethro and Sidney came in style. The Detective wore a British looking cap, much like that feller Sherlock, with a tweed jacket and his silver monocle. He was smoking from a sturdy wood pipe and walked with one paw behind his back. The Colonel, meanwhile, was decked out in his finest blue military suit, and it appeared he'd just been decorated for valor. "Well, quite a civilization you humans have managed," said the Detective, staring up at the ceiling and stained glass.

Plenty of other creatures filed in as time went on, so that by and by the hall was packed to the brim with humans and critters of every imaginable stripe and size. It was right eschatological, I wagered, and got a tear in my eye at the sight. But of course, something was missing. Bigfoot and Old Tate.

"Have you seen the Ghoul since?" I asked the two friends.

They shook their heads. "No, sir. But there have been more and more critters leaving the Gambit and surrendering themselves to the Creature Kingdom," said the Colonel.

"That's right. Something's happened over there since the battle, and it don't look so good for the powers of the gloom."

"I wonder what it could've been," I mused. "Unless . . . Bigfoot didn't actually die?"

"We can't come to many sure conclusions of the king," said the Detective, sadly. "He always was unpredictable. Irrational, some might say, but madly discerning might be a better term for it. He's got good magic up his sleeve that he's used afore to trick fools like the Ghoul into defeat." He sighed and smiled, then nodded. "We got confidence, brother Arnie. We always got confidence."

"And what of the Duke?"

Jethro grinned and winked at the Colonel. "The good Duke was last seen fleeing through the Mallard Glade, where he used to live, when he first left the Creature Kingdom."

"That's right," said the Colonel. "And we aim to search him out. That's our next assignment."

I wished them the best of luck with the endeavor and hoped for the crazy bobcat's ultimate redemption, though I knew that to be a stretch.

It was then that Mr. Ham feebly walked through the door of the chapel and faced the festival head on. He saw me conversing with the fox and jackalope, blinked at the ground, and then fell plumb backwards in a swoon! The three of us rushed over to help him up, and when he came to by and by, he found himself surrounded by the very mythical critters he'd made a profession of denouncing. "It must be the wine I drank," he whispered, sitting up and holding his head.

"Eh? There's wine here?" said the Colonel.

"It's a . . . an illusion of the psyche . . . a hallucinatory trick of the synapses," wheezed the poor professor.

"Ah c'mon, son!" I chortled, clapping him on the shoulder and leading him into the chamber. "Lookit here! The chocolate pudding Old Man Scooter makes that you like so much."

"Oh. Yes. I . . . I do quite enjoy the pudding." He kept eyeing all the critters in the room, at first in shock about how he seemed to be the only one confused by their presence. But he obediently started to eat the pudding, and take a drink of hard cider, and bite into the corn and ham, and slightly laugh at a joke that Sammie made, and then it was all over: we saw the humanity rush back into the young man like a wildfire. By the end of the evening Mr.

Ham was merry, and he sang, with the rest of the chamber, the great hillbilly hymn from which the title of this humble little book is derived:

> The hills and streams, they sing
> Of the glory and the light,
> And together our voices bring
> The song of the beautiful sight:
>
> That all of us are worth the tears,
> That each is an image of the good,
> So we cast away all the fears,
> And treat our neighbor as we should.
>
> Whatever trial may come and fall,
> Whatever tree crumbles to the ground,
> This we declare above it all,
> That we'll sing of the deeper sound.

After the song concluded, I noticed an unexpected guest in the corner of my eye. He was holding his coonskin cap in his hands, head bowed, sheepishly looking up at the crowd every once in a while. It was young Japheth, wearing an ordinary suit and tie with his hair combed and his face cleanly shaved. At first, I was surprised that he had the nerve to show himself at the party. He'd caused a lot of folks a lot of harm and had much mending to do. But I was even more surprised to find that Millie, his old lover, was the one that come up to him and throwed her arms around his neck, crying aloud and saying, "I'm sorry, Japheth! You didn't have to do nothin' to please me. I'll love you, if you'd only love me!" I suppose she'd seen the lengths of Japheth's mental and moral dissolution over the last few months and realized that she'd toyed a bit with his soul, asking him to capture Bigfoot to prove his love for her. But I knew there was an even deeper wound that feller was trying to satiate and wasn't never healed 'til Bigfoot took his place at the traitor's post. The boy's eyes were swimming with tears, and with the whole town gazing down on the sight, he gently folded her in her arms and whispered, "I love you, Millie. And *I'm* the one who ought to be sorry. Forgive me?"

"Well of course, I forgive you." And I forgave him too, I reckoned, and felt a release of joy in the doing.

Japheth went round with Millie on his arm and sat down with her family, and there warn't a feller, woman, nor child who didn't drop by his table to settle a hand of mercy on his shoulder. The boy we all used to love and look out for was back, and that shadow of a lustful, angry fur trader, full of resentment and bitterness, was well out the door and fading away.

The tables were all cleared to the edges of the room, the mead and ale barrels brought out, and the country dancing commenced. Waltzes and promenades and reels and square dances abounded through the night, all at the foot of the chapel altar and with Japheth and Millie almost always the center of the action. He didn't seem to me to be the same feller, to be straight with ye. But he was *himself,* if ye gather my meaning. It was like the Japheth that ran his brains in the ground trying to harness the nature on his doorstep, had suddenly become one with everything he had once set out to ridicule, hurt, and kill. He twirled Millie like a top, and she sunk back into his arms as the final dance concluded and the last fiddle string was broke, and the final glass of whiskey was raised and toasted and drunk. It was a night no one in that room ever forgot for as long as they lived.

That night, after everyone had gone home, I brought some fixings out to Old Tate's. His goats were shut up in their pen, and the tractor, still broke down by the shed, set washed in a floodlight. Shem had put up some twinkling Christmas lights on the gable of the doorway, and inside, a single lamp was lit right next to the old man's bed. I came in, stamped my boots, and whispered, "Tate, you old coot! You missed the banquet but the banquet ain't gonna miss you! Hehe."

"Aw shucks, son, ye ought not have come so late," he muttered. "Say, bring in the whiskey when ye come in." I entered the bedroom with the goods, handing him the plate and pouring ourselves just a smidge of the whiskey. Old Tate was sitting up in his bed, looking a bit thinned out, but rested and healthy enough at that. He chuckled, said thanks, and started to eat the meal whilst I took a seat at his bedside.

"Well, son, it seems that it's time for me to die. 'Cording to the doc."

"That's what ye said the last time I was here," I said. I sipped the whiskey.

"I know, I know. But, you know, I've thought about it for a spell, and all things considered, I don't think it'd be a bad time. I plan on leavin' the place to that young Shem. The one that's got a thing for your Sammie."

"The one who saved my rear end at that," I said. "Yes."

"That way he can start a family out here, and I'll know that it warn't no smarmy bank that took over and turned the place into a Starbucks, or some other nonsense."

"A valid concern, I'll grant you that!"

"Indeed." Old Tate finished the corn and mashed taters I'd brought him, and started to set into the ham, but then set down the fork and said, "Arnie."

"Tate."

"I must say, brother, that I'm mighty proud of you. Lord knows I wish I could've been right by your side fightin' that wicked Ghoul. And I wished I could've seen that glorious Bigfoot one last time." I scooted closer to him and we clasped hands as a tear rolled out of both our eyes at once. "So ye promise me, son, that you won't ever fall for the trick that this life is all there is, for it ain't. Now that I'm on the edge of it, I know that it ain't."

"Yessir," I said.

"And we'll see each other again, you know, by and by."

"Of course, Tate."

I don't know when exactly the old feller passed away, but I fell asleep in my chair whilst he finished his honey ham, and when I woke up, Tate was laying there with his hands joined on a chest that warn't rising nor falling. And the dishes were all neatly stacked on the bedstand.

The walk back home was a quiet, silver one. The moon and stars made the trees cast long shadows in front of me. It had snowed again, lots. As I came up past the chicken coop, feeling down and out, and yet at peace at the same time, I had the nerve to turn around and observe Scraggly Hill in the moonlight. At first there wasn't a sight nor sound to haunt the place. But as the moments passed, I'd be darned if I didn't see Bigfoot, almost taller than the trees themselves, swaying through the snow, and the figure of a limber old man jigging along behind him. "It's an ornery, wonder filled universe, Arnie Tuck!" came the laughing voice on the hill. I wasn't sure if the words came from Bigfoot, the old man, or both, but I heard them, and wouldn't forget them for the rest of my life.

Mindy opened the door and put her hand on my shoulder, and whispered, "Come to bed, honey. It's late." And when I closed the door behind me, the hill was empty, and the stars shone on.

THE END

.

Made in United States
North Haven, CT
13 August 2022